BOY NEXT DOOR

ADAM WYE

Anchor Mill Publishing

Boy Next Door

Cover image: Beach Study - Henry Scott Tuke

Anchor Mill Publishing

4/04 Anchor Mill

Paisley PA1 1JR

SCOTLAND

anchormillpublishing@gmail.com

Adam Wye

For S.G.

And the sunlight clasps the earth,

And the moonbeams kiss the sea—

What is all this sweet work worth

If thou kiss not me?

Percy Bysshe Shelley: Love's Philosophy

ONE

I topped Michael's glass of wine up. And my own. There were just the two of us. Catching up on our news and sharing a bottle or two beside the fire in what was now my house. We did this every other week. We lived next door to each other. The alternate weeks we did the same thing at his house. We had been doing this for a couple of years now. Ever since our respective partners had unexpectedly died within weeks of each other. We had grown to like each other enormously since our double bereavement. It might have seemed the most obvious thing in the world that we would eventually pair up. The problem was that, while I'd been widowed by the death of my long-time male partner, Michael had been made a widower by the death of his lady wife. I was the gay one, he the straight. We were both thirty-nine.

Michael was six foot one, and slim to the point of skinniness. His feet were on the big side and his hands and fingers long and workmanlike – in part the legacy of a misspent youth working on building-sites. A tall endomorph with long hands and feet: I couldn't help thinking that his jeans concealed something else that matched, though of course I'd never seen it. He had once told me, though, that he wasn't circumcised. I'd asked him, point-blank, when slightly drunk. 'No, I'm not,' he'd said and I'd taken his word for it. There was no earthly reason why he'd lie to me about that.

A further insight came from a conversation I'd once had with him – again we were both a little drunk – in which he told me that at the age of thirteen he'd been supple enough to bend so far as to take his dick in his mouth. I was so knocked out by this piece of information that I failed to pry out the supplementary details I would have liked to hear about. And having missed that opportunity I found that it would be a difficult conversation to revisit. Although I did think about it occasionally during subsequent conversations... When we were talking about the stock market, or our gardens, or the health of our pets. Yet I could never find a good moment to slip in those extra questions.

I once got him to put the palm of his hand towards me and I pressed mine against it. 'That's interesting,' I told him. 'Your hand's a good inch longer than mine is, and ...' I let him work out what I was getting at. Actually,' I said, withdrawing my hand so that he could withdraw his, 'the standard way to measure ... I was told ... is to reach with your middle finger down as far as you can go towards your wrist. That distance – from finger tip to the ball of your thumb or wherever – is supposed to be the length of it.' He laughed and actually carried the experiment out, bending his middle finger till it touched near his wrist. Though he made no comment on the result. I scrutinised his face carefully for any sign as to whether he thought the measurement accurate or not but couldn't read one there.

I had another go at finding out what my new best friend's dimensions were one night a few months later.

Parting in the hallway of my house with our usual chaste hug – and being fired up somewhat by a good evening's wine intake – I made a grab for his crotch. I didn't get very far, though. Michael said, 'Oy!' and wrenched himself out of our cosy embrace. 'Keep your hands to yourself!' he told me, with some annoyance in his voice, and quickly let himself out of the front door. Within minutes I'd sent him a text, apologising. I didn't get a reply, though. So in the morning I went round to his place before he left for work and said my, 'Really sorry, mate,' eyeball to eyeball with him on his doorstep. He half grinned. 'Well,' he said, 'Let's draw a line under it.' I was forgiven, I realised with a huge surge of relief.

Actually I'd taken a crazy risk with our precious, treasured friendship for very little. I might have touched his dick through his loose-fitting jeans, or I might have touched one of his balls. I'd touched something that wasn't simply his leg, certainly, but I hadn't had enough time to get a proper feel of it. So I couldn't even say with certainty what I'd been touching, let alone how big it was.

*

A couple of weeks after that last incident I got a call from Michael at ten o'clock in the evening. 'Are you up for a drive out in the snow?' was his opener.

'Erm – yes,' I said, guessing this might be some sort of emergency and wondering what it was.

'Timmy's gone off the road near the river bridge and

needs rescuing…'

'I'll be out in the driveway in one minute,' I said.

We took Michael's car: it was a 4x4 Range Rover and better at dealing with deep snow than my Audi A4 was. I threw my own snow shovel in the back alongside Michael's, noticing that he'd prudently also chucked in his towing chain.

It was snowing lightly and the road, ploughed earlier that day and so lined with a low white wall of snow on each side of it, was now once again covered with a white, inch-deep carpet. Going down the steep, winding hill towards the river we got an impression of something like the Cresta Run glistening in front of us in the headlights.

'I shouldn't have let him stay out late,' Michael said. 'In this weather.'

'Yes you should,' I countered. 'Don't beat yourself up. He's eighteen. Old enough to make his own mistakes and learn from them. You were right not to stop him going out – or staying out. Whichever.'

'I just hope he hasn't written the car off.'

'How did he sound when he called you?'

'Shaken. Unhurt, though. At least he said so.'

'Well, that's the main thing.' I stated the obvious. 'Nothing else matters.'

We saw Timmy's Mini easily. The rear half of it was still in the road, on the sharp bend on the far side of the river. The car had taken no notice of the bend evidently, as the front end of it was embedded in the white wall thrown up by the snow plough. It struck me that that white buffer might have been a godsend, preventing the car from ploughing through the thorn hedge beyond it.

By the time we pulled up Timmy had emerged from the car through the passenger door and was taking cautious steps towards us. Before either he or his father said anything they briefly embraced each other and I was touched to see that.

'Doesn't look too bad,' Michael said after quickly casting his eye over what could be seen of the Mini. Then he looked at me. 'We could waste a lot of time and energy digging round it. Maybe give it a little tug first and see if we can move it? What do you think?'

'Yep,' I said. 'Let's do that.'

Michael drove his 4x4 slowly past the half buried Mini and stopped it. He was in the middle of the road, but no traffic was passing. It didn't look like any more was going to. The three of us got the chain out and, after a bit of fiddling, found a place to attach it to the Mini. The other end went round the towing hook that the Range Rover was equipped with.

'This'll be interesting,' Michael said as he prepared to get back into his driving-seat. I saw what he meant. He would be pulling up the hill on a snow-covered surface.

'Shall we all sit in?' I suggested. 'For extra ballast.'

'Maybe,' said Michael a bit doubtfully. We got in anyway, Timmy and I, climbing into the back seat from opposite sides. Apart from anything else, I thought, we – and especially Timmy – would be warmer.

'Here goes,' said Michael, getting into gear and easing in the clutch extremely gently. Timmy and I twisted round on the seat to peer through the rear window. As Timmy's face turned past mine I caught the faintest trace of a beery sweetness on his breath. A reminder – along with the car, which was his first: he'd been driving since the summer – that this boy I'd known since he was four, was no longer the kid I sometimes still thought him. 'Are you sure you're OK?' I asked him, resisting the sudden urge to put my arm across his shoulder.

'I'm fine,' he said. 'Just a bit shaken up.'

The chain tautened and the 4x4 began to vibrate as the wheels alternately bit and spun on the snowy surface. And then, astonishingly, the Mini began to follow us, inch by inch, out of the snow heap. Timmy called, with surprise in his voice, 'It's doing it!'

'Yeah,' I corroborated. 'It's moving.' I don't think any of us had expected that. All imagining, I think, that we'd have to get back out and set to with the shovels. But now here it was – the Mini coming slowly unstuck like a tooth being pulled by a skilled dentist. We pulled it a yard out into the road, then Michael stopped his engine. We got out and went back to the Mini.

It looked fine and dandy. Its encounter with the piled-up snow had bent the number-plate a little but apart from that it wasn't even dented. We set to, clearing snow from the wheel arches and tyre-treads with whatever items came to hand – the long handles of the snow shovels poking awkwardly into the wheel arches and my pocket comb freeing the tyre treads. By torchlight we looked under the bonnet. Everything seemed normal.

'Shall I see if I can start it?' asked Michael.

'May as well,' I said. We both harboured the visceral fear that the thing might blow up as soon as he started it, though neither of us would say it. I knew Michael felt this, just as I did. Because everybody in this situation always does.

'Fingers crossed, then,' said Michael. He got into the Mini and ... started it first go. Then he got out again. Without looking at Timmy he spoke to me directly. 'How would you feel about driving it home?'

'No worries,' I said at once. I tried not to glance away at the Cresta Run winding upwards from the other side of the bridge.

'If we go first,' said Michael, 'we'll keep an eye on you behind us. We'll be in a good position to tow you if you get into trouble.' He'd made several things clear without having to say them. First, that he wasn't forbidding Timmy to drive the Mini home, but by the same token he absolutely wasn't going to let him do it.

And Timmy would be riding alongside him in the 4x4, not with me in the Mini. I was in total, though unspoken, agreement with these arrangements.

I was a very experienced driver. Even so, there can be few who would take a Mini up a snow-covered one-in-seven gradient without at least a little apprehension. At any rate the other car would be ahead of me. 'Don't bloody forget to look for me in your mirror,' I joked before getting into the driving seat.

The climb, when we did it a minute or two later (Michael had to go and turn the Range Rover in a nearby lane) was slow and a bit slithery but in the end uneventful, and the final two miles home along the flat were almost easy.

I parked the Mini behind Michael's car on his half of our shared driveway. We all got out of our doors together. 'That was really brilliant, mate,' Michael said to me. 'Big, big thanks. Want to come in for a coffee?'

'Better not,' I said, guessing – based on past experience – that the coffee would probably be turned miraculously into wine once we got into the living-room. 'Early start in the morning.'

'Well, next drink's on me then,' Michael said. 'Whenever.'

Then Timmy walked towards me between the two cars. He came right up to me and said. 'Thank you, William.' As he spoke he suddenly put his arms round me and held me very tightly and closely. I could even feel the little mound of his crotch pressed hard up against my own.

I hugged him back of course. Just for a few seconds. Then we disentangled. 'I'm just glad you're OK,' I managed to say. I wasn't at all sure that *I* was.

*

I wasn't actually sure that Timmy even liked me. Not that our paths had often crossed. He had simply been the kid next door back in the days when Aidan was alive and the two of us were, presumably, just the gay couple next door in Timmy's eyes. Aidan and I hadn't been particularly close to Michael and his wife back then. By the time of Michael's wife's death and my Aidan's death (it was only after those events that Michael and I became really close) Timmy was a typical sixteen-year-old with a typical sixteen-year-old's agenda. His father's gay best friend played no part in his life or, I presumed, thoughts. He never joined his father when Michael came round to my place for a drink, and I seldom saw him when I was in his own house. He would usually be up in his bedroom on his computer, while Michael and I had the downstairs to ourselves. Timmy would only pop down occasionally to ask a question about his homework or to ask if he could have something from the fridge. When he was younger he would sometimes pop down to ask for help with some computer problem and Michael would sort it out. These days, I was pretty sure, Michael asked Timmy for help with computer problems and Timmy would sort them out.

There had actually been one period when I felt that Timmy became positively hostile towards me. For a reason that was entirely my own fault. One summer evening about eighteen months earlier, I had been round at Michael's for drinks and, as usual, we parted with a brief hug on the doorstep. That evening we actually said our goodnights outside the front door. Not for the first time (though I had usually had a fair bit to drink when this did happen) I ended up saying, 'Sleep well, darling,' as I took my leave. Walking back to my own front door I glanced back and noticed that Timmy's bedroom light was on and his window open. He slept right over the front door. I wondered if he'd heard me calling his father darling and, if so, what he would make of it.

He had heard. And didn't think much of it. That became apparent over the next couple of months as, whenever we happened to see each other on the driveway, or over the back fence, or on his way out of his father's living room as I was on my way into it, he failed to greet me and would actually look away from me, unwilling even to make eye contact, let alone exchange a polite hallo with me. Gradually this animosity wore off and we returned to hallo-ing terms, but that was about as far as it went. Until this night. And his seismic hug.

TWO

As the days passed the hug wore off. It no longer seemed so epic. I was able to see it in perspective; to see what it meant and what it didn't. It certainly didn't mean that Timmy was sexually attracted to me. It was simply the result of the lad's relief at his rescue after a moment of fright and shock. He'd hugged one of his rescuers, his father, as soon as he arrived. What could be more natural than that he should express his thanks in the same way to his other rescuer when the time came to say goodnight and part? It was still nice, though. I knew now that Timmy didn't hate me, at least. That he'd got over the unwelcome experience of hearing me call his father darling two summers back.

Actually, I shouldn't go on calling him Timmy. That was his father's private name for him, and it had been his mother's too. His friends and everyone else knew him as Tim, and that was the way I addressed him when we spoke. I would certainly never have allowed myself to damage his cred by referring to him as Timmy in front of anybody else. Except Michael of course.

Michael, of course... I would have liked to have sex with him, if I'm honest, but of course I knew I never would. So, following Aidan's death, what did I make do with instead? A few months passed before I got the taste again but then, inevitably I did. I took to haunting the public toilets on the sea-front of the nearest town – the town in whose hospital I worked. But I soon came to think this was a dodgy idea. Too near my own doorstep. Although I was almost invisible as a radiographer – often literally so behind a mask – and also because people who have come for X-rays are usually scared stiff about something and blank out the faces around the machine – there was always a small chance that I'd be recognised, in my white-coated official capacity, by someone whose cock I'd played with, or who I'd been sucked off by, in a public convenience at the other end of the town. So I gave that activity up and took my urges to London with me instead. Sometimes I travelled up specially (it was only an hour and a half on the train) and sometimes my work took me there anyway. We radiographers were encouraged to keep abreast of new technical developments in our field and were sent from time to time to one or other of the London teaching hospitals for training days during which we could get to learn about and handle new equipment.

About a fortnight after the night of The Hug I had two such days in succession. Rather than trek home for the night in between I phoned a friend of mine – he was gay but the friendship platonic – and asked if I could stay the night on his sofa-bed. It was a not infrequent arrangement. Sometimes I would buy him dinner in the evening by way of a thank-you.

On this occasion we wouldn't be having dinner together. He was going to the theatre with a friend and would be back late. I was welcome to the sofa, though.

He would leave a spare set of keys in the usual place. I told him that was all fine, and that I'd find plenty to keep me amused during the evening. He laughed, knowing exactly what I meant by that. We left it that we might see each other before bedtime, or might coincide in the morning, or might not. If we didn't I would let myself out and post his keys through the letter-box.

I took myself off that evening to a regular hang-out of mine, a gay pub in the West End. A handsome black guy got chatting to me and we went downstairs to the basement bar, which was more dimly lit than the one at street level and had sofas. The curving sofas were already well occupied by snogging couples, but we shoe-horned our way in amongst them and got snogging ourselves. We paid a brief, joint visit to the toilets where we admired and fondled each other's cocks while we urinated. Quite a little crowd gathered to watch while we did this and we both got quite stiff, but we gave up on the idea of sharing a publicly witnessed orgasm at the urinals and returned eventually to our sofa – having to shuffle our way back into it again – to resume our more sedate kissing and cuddling.

I couldn't help noticing though, out of the corner of my eye, that right between us and the next kissing pair was sitting a lovely-looking young man in tight blue denims – and a lumberjack shirt whose main colour was red. He had moody brown eyes and a mop of dark curls. He was doing nothing except nursing a large glass of red wine and staring, unfocusedly ahead of him. No-one was cuddling him and he was cuddling nobody. That seemed an astonishing waste of a wonderful resource. He was easily the handsomest guy in the place and one of the youngest. I wanted to get hold of him but wasn't sure how I could, politely, when I was locked in an embrace with this other – perfectly nice – guy whose dick I'd been playing with.

Then fate decided to be nice to me for once. 'Sorry, mate, I've got to go,' I heard my snogging partner say. At the same time I felt him start to uncouple himself. 'Otherwise I won't make my last bus.' He had some complicated changes to make en route for his home in the suburbs and his boyfriend. He'd already told me that.

'Oh well,' I said. 'See you in here again perhaps.' I tried not to sound cheered by the news of his imminent departure. Then we disentangled ourselves completely, made more polite noises and parted with smiles and waves. I didn't get up from the sofa, though. I was sitting next to the cutest guy in the basement. It was an opportunity I had no intention of passing up.

I wasn't sure what to say to him. To the beautiful lumberjack-shirted guy I was now left sitting with. So I didn't say anything at all. I put my hand on his thigh instead.

Sometimes in my life the direct approach worked. Within a couple of seconds we were locked together and kissing each other's faces, licking each other like puppies. I felt his cock through his jeans. Difficult to tell if it was hard or not. His jeans were pretty tight. I unzipped him and pulled it   out. It was hard all right.

A moment later I felt his hands tugging my zip down. He reached inside and, like a cat scooping a goldfish from its bowl, deftly hooked my own hard cock and both my balls out. 'You're big,' he said, his lips interrupting their business with mine for just long enough to tell me that.'

'You're not so small yourself,' I said.

We just about concealed our exposed privates from the gaze of other customers with hands and sleeves. Not that anyone was that interested. They all had privates of their own – theirs and their neighbours' – to be busy with. So we were left to ourselves and to each other. In between bouts of kissing we talked.

His name was Simon. He was a medical student. He was currently working, and living in, at St Thomas's Hospital on the south bank of the Thames. I'd been there in the course of my own work. I remembered that the staff canteen had a superb view across the river to the Houses of Parliament with its towers and clock. On a meal break there was no excuse for not knowing what the time was.

He was twenty-three. He'd grown up just twenty miles along the coast from where I lived. I told him where that was. He didn't need to be told how far that was from London. 'I'd like to take you somewhere for the night,' I told him. I realised without him having to tell me, though he did tell me, that he couldn't take me back to St Thomas's. In reply I said, 'Trouble is, I'm staying the night on a friend's sofa. Not sure how he'd take it if I turned up with you in tow. I suppose we could try it…'

'Why don't you text your friend and ask?' Simon said. 'He can only say no.'

I thought this was wonderfully sensible and said so. I also thought that of course I should have come up with the idea myself. I didn't tell Simon that. 'His name's Gary,' I said as I tapped out my message. *Would it be OK if I brought a friend back? He's a medical student… but be honest!* I put the bit about Simon's professional status in order to reassure Gary that I wasn't bringing back some bit of rough trade who would trash his nice flat and disappear with both our wallets. A minute later Gary's reply came back. *Don't know how you'll fit on the sofa but that's fine.* I showed this to Simon. 'Your friend's a good mate,' he said appreciatively.

'He's a television producer,' I said. 'Not that that makes a difference to anything.'

I got us both another glass of wine from the bar, only just remembering as I stood up that something was sticking out of my fly. With some difficulty I stuffed it back inside before anyone had time to take exception to it.

A little later we made our exit. I imagined it was something like ten o'clock in the evening but when I glanced at my watch I saw it was nearly one. To my surprise there were still buses running and people waiting to board them at the stops. I'd been living a long time in the country, forgetting what big city life was like.

We sat on the upper deck of the bus, right at the front. The view of the twenty-four-seven streets, brightly lit and full of exotic bustle, was good from up there, and we could also stroke each other's legs and crotches without people noticing too much.

Gary's bedroom light was off when we got to his mews house, but he had turned the sofa into a bed for us and laid out not one but two clean towels. We were both quite charmed by that touch. Quietly we began to undress each other.

Simon was dark-haired and so was his chest. The hair on that part of him parted neatly in the middle, growing away on either side to swirl artistically and symmetrically around his by now excited nipples. His cock, which I already knew by now, was attractively shaped, uncut and tapering. I didn't get much of a chance to admire the rest of him at a distance, though. He was very heavily into kissing me and maximising our physical contact, pressing his chest and belly against mine, grinding his cock against mine and pushing his knees so firmly into mine that I had to lock them to avoid being pushed over. I was more than fine with all of this.

Eventually, though, I tore my mouth away from his and said, 'Come on, let's get into bed.' Gary's house was nicely heated. All the same it was anything but a summer night: we were barely into March. So we tucked ourselves between the duvet and the bottom sheet. I made the most of the brief moment of beauty as he climbed in beside me, before the sight of him was extinguished by the bed covers. Even now, though, he felt and smelt nice.

'I'm not sure I want to fuck,' he said. He didn't specify which way round he meant.

I was only partly disappointed by that. There was an element of relief in my response to his remark. The noise and activity that would be involved in fucking Simon or being fucked by him on what was in the end only a sofa, and just the other side of a thin partition wall behind which my more than hospitable friend lay asleep... I said, 'That's fine. I'm not sure I'm up for that either, in present circumstances.'

So we lay sort of side by side but rolled towards each other, like the two halves of a book that is being read, and wanked each other to a climax. Mine was impressive enough but he surpassed me in every particular. The tremors that ran through him were seismic, and he covered his belly with what felt like a brimming egg-cupful of spunk. We mopped ourselves up with one of the towels Gary had provided for us, grateful for his forethought. Then we settled down to sleep, my arm cradling Simon's head for most of the night. And in the morning, as soon as we awoke, we repeated the performance.

After that, though, we had to get up and go to work. Each of us heading to a different hospital in different parts of town: Simon to St Thomas's and me to the

Royal Free. Gary hadn't surfaced when, dressed, we went downstairs and made coffee, drinking it quietly in the kitchen, standing up. Then we kissed for a final minute, giving each other's semi-soft dicks a parting caress through trousers.

We walked to the tube station together, swapped email addresses and phone numbers, then made for different platforms: me to head north while Simon went south. Sitting on the train a minute later I thought about the ritual of swapped phone numbers, and hopes expressed to meet again, promises to keep in touch. They rarely came to anything after such casual encounters. One night stands tended to be exactly that.

THREE

When I checked my phone for messages one tea-time a few days later I found a request from Michael to call him.

'Cheers,' he said when I did that. 'Don't know if you could do us an enormous favour. Depends when you finish work...'

'I'm sure I can,' I said. I would have walked over broken glass for Michael, or so I'd told myself, and he was hardly likely to be asking me to do that.

'Timmy hasn't got his car today and I've got to work a bit late. If there's any chance you could pick him up from in town...'

''Course I can,' I said. I told him what time I was finishing and we arranged a time for me to pick Tim up outside the college where he studied. Some kind of computer science plus business studies, I thought. 'Any time,' I finished. 'It's a very small thing to ask.' I didn't mention the broken glass.

*

I did feel a bit uncomfortable crawling my car slowly past the front of the college, peering into groups of students who were standing about and peering back at me through my windscreen. Fortunately Tim spotted me quickly and made a beeline for my passenger door.

'It's really good of you,' he said, climbing in beside me.

'Not at all,' I said. 'I work just up the hill. As you know. What's up with the Mini?'

'It's in for its M.O.T. There's a couple of things need doing and they're keeping it in overnight.' He made his car sound like a hospital patient.

'I can take you back in, in the morning if you need me to,' I offered. 'And bring you home again. You'll be without a car again tomorrow, effectively. However early they bring it back.'

'I'm sure dad'll be able to drive me tomorrow,' Tim said.

'Poor dad,' I said. 'He's probably working in quite the opposite direction. I'll be coming into town anyway – and driving back.' I sometimes thought that Tim, the only child, was a bit over-dependent on his father for a boy who would be nineteen in another few weeks. Though I sometimes thought that over-dependency a bit of a two-way street.

Michael sold agricultural supplies to farmers and drove with samples from farm to farm. His hours could be quite long – negotiations elastic – and he needed his 4x4 with its forgiving suspension for making his way, snow or no snow, up and down farm tracks. 'Tell him I've offered, anyway,' I said to Tim. 'Mind you don't forget.'

'OK,' he said. Then he chuckled and said sweetly, 'I promise, William.'

'You can call me Will,' I said. 'Your dad does.'

Two years had passed since Tim had last sat next to me in the front passenger seat. From time to time I had run him to the bus stop, or picked him up if I passed him on the road walking back from somewhere. But this hadn't happened for a while. I was struck forcibly now by the change in his size. Back then he had been a kid sitting next to me. Small legs next to my adult ones. But now I saw his thighs the other side of the gear-lever, matching my own in length and muscular bulk. He still had more growing to do. This time next year his legs would be longer than mine, and maybe bigger. He might match his father in stature, and Michael – at six foot one – was a good three inches taller than I was.

We wound our way out through the town's outskirts. Ahead of us lay an eight-mile drive through the countryside. I felt suddenly self-conscious, a gay man sharing the intimate space of my car with a handsome youth who was the only son of my best friend. What would we find to talk about? I found myself unexpectedly tongue-tied.

Happily Tim seemed to have no similar inhibition. He began to prattle easily about the courses he was doing, about the events of that day, and about his mates. When he talked of those he mentioned them by name. They were all boys' names, I noticed. But I didn't read anything into that. If he had a girlfriend, or girlfriends, he would be unlikely to share intimate stuff about them with an outsider like myself.

His ease in my company loosened my own tongue eventually. I told him one or two of the sillier, funnier things that had happened to me during my own day at work. Including one anecdote which was a bit risqué, I thought but, emboldened by the easy-going warmth that seemed to be growing between us, I risked it. It concerned a mix-up with two sets of X-ray plates. One set had belonged to a man, the other to a woman. The two patients had the same surname and first initials. The almost inevitable shouldn't have happened, but somehow it did. Fortunately the consultants had sent the results back (with a *take a bit more care* warning) before the patients were exposed to the sight of photographs of patients that purported to be themselves, with the wrong kind of internal and external sexual parts.

Tim guffawed at that. Not, I realised, because the story was all that funny but because he appreciated the fact that I felt able to tell him it. We were two boys together now, it seemed. It was a bonding moment.

We passed the spot – the sharp bend at the bottom of the hill by the river bridge – where Tim's car had gone off the road a couple of months back. 'That was really great of you to turn out that night,' he said now, reminded of the incident.

'Of course I turned out. For you. For your dad.' I paused for a second. 'I'd do anything for him. I guess you do know that.'

'I do know that,' Tim said. It was his turn to pause. Then he said, 'It's nice.'

I was touched – even startled – by that. I felt brave enough to say, 'It's great that you're OK about your dad having a gay friend. It means a lot to me. He's the best friend I've got.'

Tim said quickly, in a no-nonsense tone that surprised me, coming so quickly after his previous remark, 'It's just as well he's got you. He's so moody he doesn't have any other friends.'

'Moody?' I queried. I was astonished. 'He's never moody with me.' With me Michael was all milk and honey, all sweetness and light. He'd never been anything else.

'That's because you're you,' Tim said in a very grown-up way. At that moment our two houses came in sight and I braked and signalled, turned into our driveway.

'I see,' I said.

Tim opened the passenger door as soon as we'd come to a stop. Before I'd turned the engine off. 'Don't forget to pass on the offer for tomorrow,' I said to his back as he started to get out. 'Both journeys. Morning and evening.'

'OK,' he said. And, 'Thanks again.' Then the door was shut and I saw his shadowy figure cross the driveway behind my car and head for his own front door.

The outside light came on automatically as he approached it. I saw him open the door with his key and disappear inside. Only then did I switch my engine off.

*

It was some hours later that my phone rang. Michael's voice. 'Tim said you'd offered... I mean tomorrow...'

'Of course,' I said. 'You don't need to ask.' I was all milk and honey. All sweetness and light. I remembered what Tim had said just as we were arriving home. *That's because you're you.* It worked both ways round of course.

I did drive Tim to college the next morning, making the little detour through the town on my way to work, and brought him back that night. We were even more comfortable in each other's company this second day, and enjoyed our homely little chats. I felt so much at ease with Tim in fact that a couple of times I very nearly patted his nearer thigh with my hand across the gear-stick and had to stop myself. When we returned home that night, though, Tim's Mini was back on the driveway. There would be no need for me to drive him back to college in the morning. I didn't see him again to speak to for a fortnight.

I saw Michael during that fortnight. Twice we had our weekly drinky evening – once at my house in front of the log fire and once at his. Among other things Michael told me of the plans for Tim's nineteenth birthday, which was looming up. Michael would be taking Tim out to a restaurant, along with his sister – Michael's sister – and her two kids, plus two of Tim's college mates. If the youngsters then wanted to go on to a club in town after that... That was fine by Michael, he said. There would be no question of any of the youngsters driving, though: he would make sure of that. It would be a taxi home – or a night sleeping over at one of Tim's mates' place in town.

I didn't offer to drive into town in the small hours to ferry Tim back. Nor was I to be invited to be part of the restaurant party, and I was fine with that. It was Tim's night – to spend with his family and friends, and I belonged to neither category. I said simply, 'Well, if the kids go on to a club and you come back on your own, by all means look in for a nightcap. You don't need to be asked.'

'Might just do that,' Michael said. 'Mind you, it's still a couple of weeks off.' And our conversation drifted away, as I put another log on the fire and Michael topped our glasses up, to the cheering fact that in just a few days' time the clocks would go forward. It was a sign of spring approaching and, even if the temperature did nothing to substantiate it, it was a thought that gave pleasure to us both.

*

There are a few days each spring and autumn, around the times when the clocks change, when people can't make their minds up, in the early evening, whether to have the lights on and the curtains drawn shut, or curtains open and the lights off. They often end up, during those few days, with lit interiors and un-curtained windows for half an hour or so at dusk. I used to enjoy those times when I lived in cities. Walking back from the bus stop, or heading out with Aidan to a restaurant or a pub, I would find myself momentarily a party to the lives of total strangers. Glancing at lit windows as I passed I would find myself seeing little pieces of those people: their tastes in furniture, their dressing gowns or towels if they had just taken a shower or a bath, even the food they were about to serve and eat.

It happened less often in the countryside. Here houses had front gardens and were screened by hedges. But it could happen at my house. It lay slightly closer to the road than Michael's and just occasionally people crossing the road in our direction would find themselves looking straight in at my front windows. Few people did that, though. Few people walked our stretch of country highway; most drove quickly past, their eyes focused on the road ahead. It generally happened only when people were coming to call on me anyway. Or on Michael.

Perhaps two days after the clocks went forward at the end of that March I was sitting in my front room shortly after coming back from work. I had the lights on already, but hadn't closed the curtains yet. I was actually winding down by looking at some porn on my laptop. In the unlikely event that somebody looked through the window they wouldn't see that, though. I was facing the windows, so they would see only the back of the laptop. I was pretty safe from prying eyes. That wouldn't have been the case if I'd already got my dick out, but I hadn't yet.

A movement outside the window caught my eye and I looked up. I saw Tim. He was crossing the road towards his own house but – probably to take advantage of a lull in the school-run traffic – he was crossing directly opposite where I sat. Our eyes met and locked. We expressed our shared surprise in quick smiles that then became grins. Tim waved his hand. I waved mine back. I made a thumbs-up sign. He made the same gesture back. The sun was still lighting the countryside outside. It shone from the side on Tim's blue eyes. I'd always known they were blue and quite big. Now for the first time I saw them as if transfigured by the moment. They were blazing blue starbursts, framed with long black lashes. His smile, and now his eyes… I realised at that moment that the kid was gorgeous.

Then something happened to his face. He didn't stop smiling; his eyes stayed wonderful and frank. But some thought that was imprisoned in his mind escaped at that moment onto his face. It wore the look of someone who suddenly thinks of saying something, then isn't sure that they really can, or should, say it.

The moment passed. He finished crossing the road and turned past my front gate towards his own house. For a few seconds I wondered if he would knock at my front door. I thought about how quickly I could switch my porn-enlivened computer screen off. But the seconds turned to a half minute, then to a minute. I didn't need to switch the laptop off. I debated with myself whether to shut the curtains on the evening sunshine or to switch my living-room lights off for privacy. In readiness for the moment, now imminent, when I would take my cock out.

FOUR

When I got an email from someone called Simon I had to think for a moment. I had a distant cousin called Simon, who I hadn't seen since I was a child. And I'd had a friend at university with the same name, though we too had rather lost touch in recent years. But then it came back. My one-night stand of a month or so back.

He was going to be in my part of the world the next weekend. Visiting his family in the town that was twenty miles along the coast. Could we meet up at some point? Twenty miles was twenty miles, but it was easily doable, as well as interesting. And, especially as he was fifteen years younger than me, it was flattering to be asked. I texted him to say yes and we arranged to meet.

It was funny to find that someone I'd met casually in a bar in London should have the same hinterland that I had. That struck me when I hesitantly named a cliff-top pub halfway between where his parents lived and where I did, thinking I'd have to give him complicated directions to it (it lay down a remote and branching track) but he told me he knew it. He also liked it and thought it a sensible place to meet. We could take it from there after that, he said. I liked the sound of that.

We met there at lunchtime. He'd borrowed his mother's car for the trip. The day was kind to us. It provided a view out over the English Channel from a height of four hundred feet. The headlands of the south coast jutted out like piers, as if striving to reach the invisible though not far-off Continent. Between them the sea swept in – in broad bays – to lick the coast. Towards the horizon the Channel lay like a tray of silver paint. We stood in the car-park looking at it together without speaking for a moment. Then I heard Simon's voice beside me say, 'This precious stone set in a silver sea.'

I warmed to him for that. 'Yes,' I said. 'Didn't Shakespeare have a knack of getting things exactly right?'

We turned and went into the pub. Ate a toasted panini sandwich and drank a local pint. Then we went for a wander down the steep paths that led up and down and around the undulating cliffs. The sea came into sight and went out of it. Sometimes the views were closed off by thickets of butter-flowering gorse. I quoted the old country saying: 'When the gorse is not in bloom then kissing's out of season.' And, heedless of other ramblers who would heave unannounced into view from time to time out of the bushes, we kissed.

I remembered now that once he got into kissing mode Simon found it hard to stop. I had to make an effort to manoeuvre him a little way off the frequented path and into a little clearing among the shrubs where no-one could see us unless they made a determined effort to come and look for us.

It was still a bit early in the year for lying down comfortably on the rabbit-bitten grass or bare earth. Furthermore there was prickly gorse everywhere and we wouldn't have wanted our naked buttocks and thighs to have come into contact with that. Let alone our dicks.

So we did the best we could. Still standing face to face we pulled our jeans down to our knees, letting our cocks spring out, and pulled our shirts up. We pushed our crotches, cocks and bellies into each other's, letting our hips gyrate gently, until the urge to do more than that grew strong in us and we knew we had to bring each other off before we burst.

When it came to whose turn to come would be first I bowed before Simon's relative youth. Quite literally. I crouched down, holding onto his two hands to balance myself, and took his handsome cock in my mouth. I didn't think it would be long before he climaxed and it wasn't. I felt his hips go into spasm after I'd pumped him with my lips and tongue for about a minute and then could feel the pulsing of his dick as he emptied his store of semen in my mouth. I swallowed as much as I could of him. I felt pretty safe in doing that. He was a doctor, or about to become one: I was pretty sure he took good care of his sexual health.

Sometimes it turns out that sex partners who are younger than you are feel under no social obligation to reciprocate. But Simon behaved impeccably when it came to this. Despite being satisfied himself he bobbed down – still with jeans at half-mast and with half-mast cock still drooling semen threads – and took my own, now very big, dick in his mouth. He went at it doggedly for a couple of minutes, then – I didn't want to make this into an endurance test for him – I helped things along a bit with the power of my own will and thoughts. Soon I felt myself starting to let go, and gave him a verbal warning. 'Uuh... Just about to shoot,' I said. To give him a chance to take his mouth away from my cock. But he kept on going sportingly as I tensed and then relaxed, as my sperm flooded his mouth. Though after the initial bomb-burst he did release my cock from his mouth, coaxing the remnants out of my cock with his hand while spitting out the substantial load he'd taken in his mouth. I was touched by his insistence on seeing the job through to the end and not at all offended by his spitting my semen out. After all, I wasn't a doctor, and this was only the second time we'd met.

We pulled our jeans up and stuffed ourselves back inside them, then kissed while tucking in our shirts. Back on the cliff path we headed back up to the car-park. 'Have you got time to come and see my place?' I asked.

'How far is it?'

I told him.

He looked at his watch. 'Yes,' he said. 'Let's go for it.'

'I'll take you in my car,' I said. 'Drop you back here later so you can pick your mother's car up.'

So we made the twenty-five minute drive back to my house. As I drove I did what I hadn't dared to do when Tim was my passenger. I rested my hand on Simon's thigh and slowly stroked it. I was pleased and touched when Simon crossed his arm over mine near the gear-lever and did the same thing to my leg. This is always nice when you're driving with someone you like. But it's more comfortable and less dangerous if your car is, as mine was, an automatic.

As we went we talked about ordinary, quite boring matters. We compared the two hospitals we worked at. He knew something about mine – he'd been born less than twenty miles from it – just as I knew a bit about St Thomas's. We talked about their respective facilities, their (very different!) budgets and the kind of patients they catered for most. All very boring stuff, except between people who worked in the same field. I couldn't help noticing as we chatted that we were talking the way new friends do; not simply in the way of people who've only hooked up in order to have sex together. I wondered if there might be any mileage in this

Half a mile before we arrived home I spotted Tim walking along the road, on the other side, towards his – and my – house. Perhaps he'd walked to the shop or been somewhere on a bus. I stopped and wound the window down. 'Want a lift?'

He quickly dashed across the road and was immediately in the rear seat. I introduced him to the back of Simon's head as I started off. I told Tim that Simon was a doctor friend, told him where he worked, and that we'd just had lunch together. I thought that was about enough for Tim to be going on with.

When we came to a halt on the driveway Tim very quickly opened the rear door and hopped out from the back seat. That was a trait he'd learnt or inherited from his father. Whenever Michael arrived home or parked anywhere he'd be out of the car almost before the engine had time to stop. I noticed now that Simon turned his head attentively to the wing mirror as he said a polite, 'Cheers,' to Tim while the boy got out. As soon as Tim's door was shut, and before I opened mine or Simon opened his, Simon said, 'My God, what gorgeous eyes that guy's got. Have you ever noticed?'

'Yours are pretty good too,' I said smoothly. 'Though, yes, of course I have.' I'd already told Simon in the car that Tim was my next-door neighbour. Now as we got out of the car and went into my house I expanded on that a bit. 'He lives alone with his father. The mother died around the same time that my partner Aidan did. She was very beautiful. Tim gets his eyes mainly from her. Although…' I hesitated, not sure how far I wanted to go down this route. 'Although some of that depth in them, the smoulder, comes from the dad. Michael. He and I – Michael, I mean – are very close. I'm a little bit in love with him to tell the truth.'

'Hang on,' requested Simon. 'In love with the son? Or with the father?'

'Sorry,' I said. 'I meant the father. And that's all I would have meant until a few months back. Remember all that snow we had…?'

As I showed Simon around the house and garden, while he made appreciative noises at appropriate moments, I told the story of recent events with Tim. The car in the snowdrift. The unexpected hug. The companionable drives between home and college. The extraordinary look that had appeared on Tim's face when he'd eyeballed me through my front window a week ago...

We saw the downstairs first. I made a cup of tea. We drank it as we walked round the small but busy garden. Then we went upstairs... Simon gave an appreciative pat to the double bed in the main bedroom, then inspected the bathroom and shower. 'Don't suppose we could share a shower together?' he asked brightly. 'My nether regions are caked with spunk.'

I laughed. 'So are mine, I think. Sure, we'll have a shower together.' For the second time since lunch we both began to undress.

I had one of those glass-fronted, glass-sided shower cabinets that are like a reptile tank. It was newish and nice. Although I had fantasised about sharing it with Michael some time, imagining that he might have a problem with his water-heater one day and need my help, I hadn't actually been in it with anyone else since Aidan died. This new and unplanned event was very nice.

I still remember the sight of his elegant feet, one on the outside of each of my clamped together pair, and the water cascading down on all sides of our two handsome pairs of legs. It was convenient that, though differently aged, we were almost exactly the same height.

What with our exertions, and the running water and the shower gel Simon ended up with a hand full of what looked and felt like shaving foam, or the kind of cream that is squirted from a can in restaurant kitchens. We both looked at it and laughed and commented. Then I said, 'Come on, let's get out of here and dry ourselves. Then you can give me a proper fuck on the bed... If you've time, that is.'

He'd taken his watch off to shower, so had no way to check. 'Yes,' he simply said.

After we'd dried each other we threw ourselves onto my bed and I reached down for the packet of condoms I kept in the bedside locker. I might have been confident in my medic friend's attention to his own safety but I wasn't going to give hostages to fortune. He rolled the condom onto his shapely dick without protest.

I let him do the flower arranging. He turned me onto my side and snuggled himself behind me, getting into position number whatever-it-was while he cleared his way in with a familiar finger. He may have been a good bit younger than me but he didn't seem to lack experience. Then, hooking one leg over my thigh like someone starting to mount a motor-bike he eased his way into me with all the deftness of a surgeon. I remembered that I hadn't yet asked him what speciality he intended to go in for. This probably wasn't the moment, though. I would ask him another time.

When, a short time later we had both managed another climax Simon said that, reluctantly, he would need to get back to his parents' house for supper.

We didn't shower again – that could have got us onto a never-ending cycle – but cleaned our bits together, side by side at the wash-basin, then dressed and headed out.

Who should we meet on the driveway, though, but young Tim, stowing something in the back of his father's Range Rover. We couldn't pretend we hadn't seen each other, and it would have been rude to ignore each other. We all said, 'Hi,' then Tim – perhaps a sudden nervousness making him feel that he ought to say something – addressed Simon with, 'Short visit – or are you coming back later?' I could see from his face after he'd spoken that he realised that his nerves had made him much too forward.

To spare his blushes – his cheeks were displaying a real crimson one – I said quickly, 'I've got to get Simon home to his parents. We left his car at the pub we had lunch at. But I'm sure he'll be back again before too long.' Back for more, I thought, and almost said it. But I was glad on reflection that I hadn't. One person being a bit too forward by accident was a situation that could be salvaged. Had I gone there too it might all have become a bit uncomfortable rather quickly.

I drove Simon back to where his mother's car was sitting and we parted with quite an intimate kiss in the pub car-park. We said, 'See you again soon, I hope,' and things of that sort. Then we waved to each other while Simon's car receded up the track then disappeared. A moment later I followed. I didn't see him again at the Tjunction, where he had just turned left. I turned right and headed back home again with quite a bit to think about.

I quite expected to find Tim out on the driveway when I turned down onto it. Out at the front on some pretext or other – cleaning his windscreen or checking his oil-level. But there was no sign of him. At first I thought I was quite relieved not to have to greet him and talk to him. But after a moment I realised that I wasn't relieved at all but disappointed.

FIVE

A couple of days later I stopped off at the shop in the village on my way home from work. I'd forgotten to get milk when I'd done my weekly shop and I needed to remedy the oversight. It was pouring with rain when I got out of the car so I ran into the shop. A Mini was parked outside but I didn't stop to read the registration plate nor did I give any thought to whose it might be. But when I got inside, there he was, just coming away from the counter, heading towards the door. He would need to squeeze past me to get to it.

'I thought you did all your shopping on line,' I joked.

He grinned. 'I had to call in for some stamps.'

I pursued my weak joke. A bit relentlessly perhaps. 'Stamps? Things of the past for you lot, I thought. Email? Text?'

'Yeah,' he said. 'But it's for legal stuff. Official documents.' He sighed and grimaced, his eyebrows going up.

I didn't question him about the documents of course. They might be to do with insurance or financial business. He was a fellow adult after all and it was no concern of mine. 'Well, good luck,' I said. Absurdly. Who needs to be wished luck on a purchase of some stamps?

'Cheers,' he said, and – for we'd stopped in our tracks for the duration of that little conversation – we began to move past each other. But then he stopped again and, by now almost looking over his shoulder at me, asked in a different tone of voice, a quieter one, almost urgent with curiosity, 'Was that your new boyfriend the other day?'

'Simon?' I queried. 'No. He's someone I met in a pub in London.' I found my peripheral vision rapidly checking there was no-one close to us in the shop. I dropped my own voice to a near-whisper as I said, 'Just for sex.'

By now we were facing each other again, having made a half turn around each other. Tim giggled, right in my face. 'That's what I thought,' he said. There was a grin on his face. A grin of complex origins, I thought.

'Don't get wet,' I said as he turned towards the door again.

'See ya soon,' said his departing back.

'Cheers,' I said to it.

I had to collect my thoughts. What had I come in for? Milk. I moved towards the chiller cabinets. Three days ago I'd restrained myself from saying that Simon might be *coming back for more*: that I'd be pushing the boundaries of my familiarity with Tim beyond acceptable limits. But now I'd just told him straight out that our relationship was all about sex. What a difference three days make.

*

I had to think about Tim's forthcoming birthday. Usually I simply dropped a card through the door. This year, though, I knew him slightly better... Perhaps a small present? I didn't want to overdo it. His father and I restricted ourselves to giving each other a bottle of wine on birthdays. A fairly expensive, non-everyday bottle, admittedly, but still just a bottle. Nothing big. Maybe a bottle of wine would be appropriate for Tim. But I'd never had a sit-down meal with him, never seen him in a pub. I'd never seen him with an alcoholic drink in his hand in his father's house. Perhaps he didn't drink. Oh, but yes he did. I remembered the sweetly beery smell of his breath on the night he'd crashed his Mini. When we'd sat together on the Range Rover's back seat... Still, perhaps his over-protective father wouldn't think a gift of wine appropriate...

I phoned Michael. Asked him what he thought. Asked him if Tim enjoyed a drink. I didn't mention the beery breath of that winter night.

'He does drink,' Michael said. 'But not a lot. Unlike some of his mates. But he'll have a beer if he's out with them. Wine too he's OK with. But don't feel you have to do anything. Get him a bottle of wine if you really want to. But certainly don't get an expensive one. He'd be embarrassed.'

'Unless he's already heavily into it he'd hardly know whether it was expensive or not,' I countered. 'But I take the point. Thanks for the advice. And don't forget, if

46

you're at a loose end at the end of his birthday evening, you're welcome to drop in to mine for one.'

'Might do. See how it goes. Cheers, mate.'

I got a bottle of Brouilly, one of the Beaujolais villages. And a card. On which I wrote the bare minimum. I didn't want to embarrass Tim by being close-up or affectionate. I took card and bottle round to his front door on the morning of his birthday before driving off to work, intending simply to leave them on the step unannounced. Tim's Mini was still on the driveway. I presumed that – if he was going to college at all that day – he hadn't gone yet.

I bent down to lay my offering on the doorstep and as I did so the door opened in my face. I straightened up and found myself eye-balling Tim. Actually we weren't eye to eye. He was standing inside the house and up a step. My eyes were level with his chin. In order to meet his eye I had to look up. 'Happy birthday, mate,' I said. I bent down again and picked the card and bottle up. I handed them up to him. 'For drinking later,' I said. 'Not recommended for breakfast.'

He chuckled, but only for half a second. The next instant he had stepped out of his front door and, on my level now, thrown his arms around me, card in one hand and bottle in the other, and buried his head between my shoulder and my neck. Because this was the second time it had happened I was not as startled as if it had been the first. The spontaneous gesture gave me an enormous jolt of pleasure – and other more complex emotions –

nonetheless.

I returned his hug, and momentarily ruffled the thick hair of the top of his head. Then, as quickly as it had begun, the moment was ended. 'Time I headed off to work,' I said. I could feel myself smiling in an abandoned, heart-on-sleeve way that he might have found disproportionate. Only... he was smiling at me in the same abandoned, heart-on-sleeve sort of way. I might have thought that disproportionate. I wouldn't have cared an atom if I had.

'And I've got to get to college soon,' he said.

'Have a good day then,' I said. I made myself turn away then, not daring to imagine what might have happened if I hadn't, and walked to my car, got in it and drove off. I didn't dare look to see if he was making his way to his own car or had gone back into the house. I sprinted off down the road. I couldn't have borne seeing his Mini in my mirror, him following me all the way to the town.

*

It's not a comfortable way to spend an evening alone: waiting, or half-waiting for someone who might call in late on for a nightcap – or might not. You don't want to spend the evening drinking and find yourself rolling to the door to greet them. What is the earliest you can consider going to bed? Entertain them in your dressing gown? Michael and I had often made maybe-yes-maybe-no late-night calls on each other over the years. It had always been nice when it had happened, and a bit of a let-down when it hadn't. Neither of us had ever entertained the other in a dressing gown.

I left the outside light on anyway that evening, to show Michael I was still up and that he could look in if he wanted to. By eleven fifteen I'd more or less given him up but then I saw his headlights sweeping into the driveway. Five minutes later the doorbell rang. And when I opened the door there he was, spot-lit by the outside light and framed by the door against the darkness.

'Bit late, aren't I?' He grinned a mixture of hope and apology. 'Your light was on…'

'You're not late at all,' I said. 'Come on in.' I let him precede me through the hall and into my living-room, where he installed himself in the armchair he usually sat in, without needing to be asked, on one side of the log fire.

'There's some red open,' I said.

'That's fine,' he said. 'Just a brief one.'

I fetched bottle and glasses, put them on the coffee table that sat between the two fireside armchairs and sat down in the vacant chair. The room also contained a big sofa, but we never sat together on that. I poured out. 'Cheers,' I said. 'How was the birthday dinner?'

It had all gone very nicely, Michael told me. Tim's two friends had turned out to be an entertaining pair, and the younger cousins had behaved impeccably. The party had only broken up thirty minutes earlier. Michael's sister had taken her youngsters home with her, and Tim and his two friends had gone off to a club in a taxi. Michael had driven home alone.

Home to me. I didn't allow myself to imagine that was how he saw it.

We talked of other things. The routine catchings-up of neighbours. About the waste-disposal people. About the local shop and its shortcomings. Gentle gossip about the lives of local people we knew or knew of. I was glad to steer the conversation away from Tim. I didn't want his father to think I was too interested in him.

But Tim did get another name check later. (We'd finished that half-empty bottle by now, and opened another.) The subject was brought up by Michael. 'Timmy met a friend of yours, he told me. Cheers for the lift in the car you gave him.'

'Any time,' I said. 'The friend was Simon. Actually one of my London … acquaintances…'

'London pickups.' Michael sniggered and his eyes gave me a mischievous twinkle.

'I didn't tell Tim *that*,' I said in laughing protest, although that was exactly what I had done. 'Turned out he comes from near here. His parents live at Westbourne. We both work in hospitals. He's a medical student.'

'Student?' queried Michael. 'How old, then?'

'Twenty-three,' I said.

'Hmm,' said Michael appreciatively. 'Well done, mate. Good to know you can still pull 'em.'

'I'll drink to that,' I said. 'Though actually,' I said, a new thought striking me, 'we haven't raised a glass to the birthday boy yet. Better toast him in his absence.' I looked at my watch. 'Just in time. Before midnight.' I raised my glass and clinked it against Michael's. 'To Tim,' I said simply.

'To Timmy,' said Michael.

I couldn't resist. I repeated it back to him. 'To Timmy.'

But then I had to make an effort to wrench the conversation away from the subject of my best friend's son again. I was curious to know whether it had been arranged that he would come home by taxi in the small hours or stay the night in town with one of his mates. With one? With both? I had to bite back all these questions and nip my growing curiosity in the bud.

During the last three years I'd grown increasingly aware that Tim didn't seem to have a girlfriend. When he was sixteen that had hardly been anything to wonder at, especially as we lived in remote countryside. But now – with Tim already mobile thanks to the Mini, and ready to head off to university within a few months – the absence of any female company around my friend's son had become more obvious.

In moments of candour – alcohol-inspired, no doubt – Michael and I had traded accounts (cautious and edited though these were) of our early sexual experiences. We'd both started in our teens, we soon discovered, although Michael had gone down the straight track and I the gay one. I couldn't help noticing – although my observations might have been inaccurate: there might have been evidence I'd had no sight of – that Tim did not seem to have followed in his father's precocious footsteps. I'd never shared these musings with Michael. Coming from the gay next-door neighbour they would have been equally unwelcome whether they hit the nail on the head or fell wide of the mark.

Though I do remember that a couple of years earlier Michael had himself mused aloud in my company on the subject of having gay offspring. This had come up in the context of a frank conversation about my relations with my own parents. My coming out to them had been difficult and fraught – I'd opened myself up to Michael on this subject. Although in time my own parents had come to accept my gayness and been supportive... I remember that Michael had said – in a gesture of support to me, I later realised – 'I've no reason to think Timmy's gay. Every reason not to. The way him and his mates talk about girls... I've heard them. But if he were, I mean *if* he was, well of course I'd be totally supportive.' I'd been glad to hear him say that and had said so. Ever since then I'd remained glad that he'd said it. I'd never forgotten that conversation.

I made an effort to bring my drifting thoughts back to the conversation that was now in progress. 'It's no good doing it just once,' I said. We were talking about killing off weeds that grew between garden paving slabs by spraying them. 'You have to do it regularly. Otherwise you'd use your time better by cutting out the roots inch by inch with a pen-knife.'

Michael sighed. 'You're probably right. Anyway, time to be off. Early start in the morning. Tim said he'll be staying in town tonight with Tyler. But I'd better be at home just in case he changes his mind.'

You don't have to be at home for him, I thought. He has his own key. He's nineteen. He can look after himself... There was no way I was going to say this.

And – Tyler, I thought. Tyler...

We stood up together and walked out into the hallway. I put my arms round Michael as I always did, and he wrapped his round me. I reached up a little with my lips and chastely kissed the cheek he turned towards me. The first time I'd kissed him, two years before, he'd been mightily shocked; had said, 'Hey!' and had rubbed at the spot as if he'd been bitten by un unpleasant insect. But over time he'd grown more used to it. He'd come to accept my occasional kiss with a good grace. At first I'd had to stand on tiptoe to deliver the salutation but these days I no longer had to. That must have meant that he bent down to receive it. I could only surmise this; there was never a witness to corroborate it.

Tonight I briefly grazed his soft cheek with my lips. I didn't hang about. I didn't want to outstay my welcome. I just had time to catch the soft feel of him and the soft smell of his beautiful face. Then I let him go, like a wonderful fish that the rules of the angling club require you to return to the water to swim away from you.

He walked out through the doorway. I stood in it and we exchanged the final traditional farewells that we had made ours over the months and years since two deaths had thrown us together. *Take care. Sleep well. See you soon. Next time...* Et cetera. Then I said, 'Maybe one day you'll actually return one of my kisses.'

'Nah,' he said. 'Don't think I'll be doing that any time soon.'

'OK,' I said but, undaunted, added, 'Maybe you'll give me a kiss on my deathbed?'

'All right,' he conceded, with something in his laughing voice that I can't find a name for but which was gorgeous. 'OK. I'll kiss you on your deathbed.'

'Good,' I said. 'That'll give me something to look forward to.'

We chuckled together. He walked round the corner of my house, a tall silhouette, and disappeared across the driveway to his own house. I didn't go to the corner to watch him get there. But I stood on the doorstep waiting till his own outside light came on automatically as he approached. Then I knew he'd made it safely. I went back indoors and turned my outside light off.

And the sunbeams clasp the earth

And the moonbeams kiss the sea –

What is all this sweet work worth,

If thou kiss not me?

SIX

I got a phone call from my London friend Gary. I hadn't seen him since I'd stayed on his sofa with Simon that time – actually I hadn't seen him for a month or two before that – and except for a quick exchange of texts – *Thanks for last night, the twin towels were appreciated. / That's fine, no worries* – the day after, we hadn't been in touch since. That was actually what Gary was phoning about. It was time we got together over lunch or something, he said. We arranged to meet in London a couple of Saturdays ahead.

Gary asked if I'd seen any more of Simon. I said that, yes, rather to my surprise I had. I told him about our cliff-top lunch and that he'd been to my house. 'He actually met Michael's son Tim twice,' I said. Gary had met Michael a couple of times on his own visits to my place. He had never met Tim but knew who he was. I told him about the brief ride in the car, but gave no details beyond that. They could keep till we had lunch together.

*

I had the afternoon off. I had done some work in the garden at the back, some horticultural spring cleaning, and then turned my attention to the small strip I had at the front, next to the road. I could see Tim's car parked on the driveway. No college for him today evidently. Michael's car wasn't there though: presumably he was still out at work.

Tim came into my field of vision, coming out of his own place and walking up onto the road. He had a letter in his hand. There was a post box just a hundred yards away so I had a pretty good idea what he was going to do with the letter. He saw me, and smiled and said waved to me.

'Hi,' I said. I pointed to the letter he was carrying and said, 'Nothing quite like the old way of doing things.' He grinned but didn't say anything in reply to that. He carried on past my picket fence towards the post box and I bent back down again to give my weeds my full attention. About a minute later Tim came walking back, minus the letter. He stopped when he got up to me, just a yard away, the other side of the picket fence. He beamed a quick smile at me, then flicked it off suddenly, as if it had been a torch. Now with an earnest, anxious look on his face he said, 'Could I talk to you, Will?' His tone of voice was troubled and untypically hesitant.

'Of course,' I said lightly. I wanted to convey that it was no big deal, him wanting to talk to me. 'Do you want to come in?'

He already knew the geography of my house. Though he hadn't been inside it for a few years he'd come in often enough when he was younger to know his way around it. 'Have a seat,' I invited casually as soon as we were in the living-room. Without hesitation he plonked himself down on the sofa, sitting right up one end of it. 'Would you like some tea   or coffee?' I asked.

'No… No thank-you,' he said.

'Whisky?' I offered with a not quite poker face.

The laugh with which he responded to that chased away the anxious look from his face and I was glad about that. 'No,' he said. 'Not yet.' We could find out how seriously to take the 'not yet' in due course. I sat down on the other end of the sofa, right up the other end, leaving a decent eighteen inches between our knees.

'When did you first know you were gay?' Tim asked.

It was only then I realised that deep down I'd been expecting the question for weeks now and had already prepared myself to answer it.

'It's a simple enough question,' I said. 'But the answer's not quite so straightforward. In a way perhaps I always knew. I've always been the person I am. But I didn't want to be gay when I was a teenager. I don't think many people actively want that. So that complicates the answer to your question a bit. But I think I'd come to accept that I was gay, and couldn't do much about it, by the time I was twenty.'

Tim had listened intently, nodding as he took in the implications of what I'd been saying. Now he looked me in the eye – a wonderful flash of blue – and said, 'You couldn't do much about it… Did you try to do something about it?'

I smiled. 'A little. I went out with a few girls when I was first at uni. Only about three. I never went to bed with any of them. But they all ended up as good friends. Just never more than that.' I paused and drew breath. 'I'd had some experience with boys at school.' He could take that or leave it. 'Then in my last year at university I went to bed with a boy of my own age and fell in love with him.' How to say the next bit? I did it as gently as possible. 'It didn't last for ever. It wasn't Aidan.'

'How old were you when you met Aidan?'

'Twenty-four,' I said. 'We had twelve years together. It can happen.'

I didn't need to ask him why he was asking these questions. I sat quietly and let him lead the conversation where he wanted it to go. I could see him thinking, planning his route carefully as he went along, like someone stepping through a quagmire.

'You must miss Aidan terribly,' he said.

'It's true,' I said.

'You must want someone to replace him. Sorry. That didn't sound too good.'

'I knew what you meant,' I said. 'And I do. Not to replace him exactly. He was a unique person. I can't find another Aidan. But I'm not going to go hunting too desperately. That doesn't work out very well usually. Either someone special will come into my life one day and they'll be the right person, or they won't.'

'I hope they will,' he said, looking into my eyes so

genuinely that it gave me a pang. Then to my astonishment he reached out and clasped my hand. I'd carelessly left it lying about, next to my knee, on the sofa. 'I think I may be gay,' he said, looking terribly worried as he said it.

'I thought you might be going to say that,' I said. 'But cheer up.' I squeezed his hand lightly. 'It won't be the end of the world if you are. And anyway, you may not be. It took me a few years to sort myself out, like I told you. I think that's quite usual. Lots of people think they might be gay when they're your age. Most of them aren't, actually.'

Tim looked displeased by this. 'I don't want it to take years to sort itself out. I don't want life to be so complicated.'

Oh my darling, I wanted to say. I wanted to scoop him into my arms and smother him with kisses and ask him to be mine for ever. It was only with the greatest effort of will that I managed not to. 'Oh Tim,' I did say. 'You know life's complicated. You're old enough to know that. You know there's nothing any of us can do about it.'

He managed a little twist of a smile. 'I suppose I do, Will.' I saw there were tears in his eyes. We both chose to pretend there weren't.

'What makes you think you're gay?' I asked. Perhaps I shouldn't have done. I hadn't meant to lead the conversation. 'Sorry,' I said. 'That was intrusive of me.

Forget I asked you.'

'It's OK,' he said. 'It's only fair. I've been asking you personal questions. I fancy some of my friends – my male friends. I don't fancy the girls I know.'

'Some people might tell you, "You haven't met the right girl yet". I'm not saying that's the right interpretation. Only that it could be.'

He ignored that. He had found his own agenda. 'The night of my birthday, I stayed in town with my friend Tyler. We had sex together.'

'Well, that's very nice,' I said. 'A perfect eighteenth birthday present, I'd have thought, from one friend to another.'

He didn't look convinced. 'It was nice in a way, and yet it wasn't. He wanted to do some things I didn't.'

'That's also very usual. And you found the experience unsettling and disturbing. Is that right?'

'How do you know that?' he asked me.

I couldn't help laughing a little. 'Take a look at me. I'm twenty years older than you or Tyler. That's how I know. Because I've been there.'

'I wish I had your experience,' he said. 'Then I'd know what I'm doing.'

'Then you'd also have lines on your face where I've got them and you haven't. And a few grey hairs around the temples. You can't have it both ways.'

I found myself looking at his crotch. In his tightish jeans it mounded slightly. I gave his hand another little squeeze. Then he did something. His fingers started to play with my fingers.

Neither of us spoke. The moment was too extraordinary. I couldn't imagine what either of would have said if we started speaking. Neither could he, evidently. So we didn't. The moment grew longer, time became elastic. We just continued to play with each other's fingers.

Eventually I knew what would be said next, and who would have to say it. Me. 'Do you want a hug, Tim?' He simply nodded.

We found ourselves somehow together in the middle of the sofa. Twisted towards each other and hugging. Our legs remained side by side, stiffly neutral, as though they didn't want to know what our torsos were doing. But then that changed after a minute… Though in the meantime, the wonder of that minute… There are moments in life when the roasted chicken lands squarely in your mouth. But then you have to think very carefully, and *be* very careful, about what you are going to do with it.

Tim did the next thing. He crossed one of his legs over mine. After a couple of seconds he must have realised that wasn't very comfortable. One of his options would have been to take that leg of his away again. But he went for the other option. Twisting himself further towards me he brought his second leg over to join the first one.

At that point I could have reached into his crotch more easily than into my own. But I did the other thing. I extricated his face from where it had been burrowing at my collarbone and kissed it.

I didn't force my tongue down his throat; just kissed his lips slowly. With his eyes closed now he kissed my lips too. His tongue made no appearance either, but he was clearly thinking hard about the moment – and tentatively savouring it.

I couldn't resist now. I felt gently at the mound in his jeans. Found the ridge of his trapped cock. It felt fairly stiff. It wasn't big. I made that discovery with no sense of disappointment. I was in awe of what was just happening. So was Tim clearly. Yet he wasn't too awestruck to worm his hand beneath his own leg to find my own equally trapped and equally stiff, but somewhat larger, member. He rubbed at it exploratively through the denim.

Then, like a cat that has suddenly had enough cuddling, he pulled himself off and away from me and retreated back to his end of the sofa. 'Sorry,' he said. 'It's just all a bit…'

'I know,' I said gently. 'I know it is.'

I sat back calmly, not saying more, not pursuing him. I waited to see if he would bolt for the door suddenly like a rabbit, or say something. For a while he didn't seem to know which of the two he was going to do, either. But then he spoke. 'I don't know whether I ought to come out to people. To dad, especially. And what to say to them. To him.'

'If I were you,' I said carefully, 'and you can take this or ignore it, I wouldn't say anything to him for the moment.' I knew I had set foot onto a minefield. 'Partly for his sake. If or when you do tell him you think you may be gay it's going to mean a bit of mental and emotional adjustment for him. But you say you're not sure yet... Well, if you had to tell him in a year or two that actually you're straight... Then there'd be another difficult conversation and another adjustment for both of you.'

'I sort of see...' he said doubtfully.

'I can tell you one thing,' I said. 'If you can bear to listen. Your dad told me once – this was more than two years ago – that he had no reason to think you were gay but that if that was how things turned out ... he'd be totally supportive.'

I could see relief flood through him. Though he said, 'But if I didn't tell him, wouldn't that be like living a lie?'

'Not for the present,' I said. 'At the moment it's an entirely private matter. Between yourself and any other person you may get involved with. We all have private business. Example...' I cast about me. '...We don't tell everyone who we vote for. It's not living a lie simply because we don't shout the information from the rooftops.' I thought of another example. 'We don't tell everyone we meet how big our dicks are. We let people know if they seem interested and if we have a good reason to want to tell them. Or if they discover for themselves.' I looked at him mischievously, inviting him to lighten up a bit.

Which he did. He chuckled. But then he looked serious again. 'Yours is massive. Did mine seem very tiny?'

'It's the normal size for your age,' I said. 'It'll probably go on growing till you're in your twenties. In any case I thought it absolutely perfect.' I was tempted to go on and say I hoped I'd get a proper look at it sometime but I didn't. The moment was too delicate. The line of contact between us was spider-silk thin and could have snapped with any rough handling.

'Thank you,' Tim said. He looked relieved by what I'd told him. Then he looked about him. 'I think I'd better go. Dad'll be back from work soon. He'll think it odd if I appear from your place.'

'Understood,' I said. 'Before you go, though… Any time you want to come in and talk again, just do it. Ring the doorbell. Also, I'll give you my email.' I picked up a pen and a scrap of paper from the coffee table and wrote it. Then I tore the paper in two and gave him both halves together with the pen. 'Write yours for me.' He did so. While he was doing it I added, 'If you don't want to talk again that's fine too. Just think about what I said about not being in too much of a rush to tell your father. And – most important of all – if you have anal sex with anyone wear a condom, just as you would with a woman. And don't let anyone do it to you unless they're wearing a condom.' I took hold of his chin and turned him to face me squarely. 'Promise?'

He grinned at me. 'Thank you, Will. I promise. Not that I plan to have anal sex with anyone. That was rather the issue with Tyler.'

'Yes,' I said. 'I rather guessed it was.'

We both stood up and I walked out into the hallway with him. Before I opened the front door for him we spontaneously hugged each other. I was shaken by how similar this felt to my regular late evening farewells with his father. But there was a difference. I kissed Tim's lips briefly, not his cheek as I did with Michael. And unlike Michael he returned the intimacy.

I walked back into my living-room completely dizzy and disoriented. I felt I was walking – slowly but buoyed up – as if the room was full of water. The difference the past half hour had made to my world was just as major.

Before I could think what I would do in the next hour or minute my phone went in my pocket. I answered it and it was Simon.

SEVEN

Simon was phoning to say that he'd be down at his parents' on Saturday – just two days away – and could drive over to me if I wanted. I said that I did want that. That it would be lovely. We reconfirmed the time of his arrival on Saturday – borrowing his mother's car again – and we finished the call.

I didn't see Tim between our earth-shaking encounter on Thursday afternoon and Simon's arrival at midday on Saturday. But Simon did. It was the first thing he told me after I'd welcomed him in and we'd kissed in the hallway. 'I saw Tim as I was getting out of the car,' he said. 'He looked a bit surprised to see me.'

'Did you greet each other?' I asked.

'We said hallo and half-waved politely. He wasn't over-enthusiastic.'

'I see,' I said. Though exactly what I saw I wasn't really sure about.

I had prepared a light lunch for the two of us but at that moment eating it didn't seem to be the thing we wanted to do first. We went straight upstairs instead and took our clothes off.

This was the third time I had seen Simon erect and naked. Again I was stirred, excited by his handsomeness. His lovely hirsute chest, the hair funnelling down through his dark treasure trail towards his bush and standing penis. That organ beginning to show its pink tip through the flute of his foreskin, like a large-scale lipstick…

I placed my hand on Simon's flat belly and ran it downwards. Slowly I enfolded his sturdy, tapering penis. 'Can I return the compliment you paid me last time?' I asked him.

'You mean fuck me?' He half grinned shyly.

'Can I?'

'Yes,' he said.

'I'll wear a condom.' I reached down for the packet in the bedside locker. By the time I stood up again Simon was already in position for me: face-down on the bed-cover and gently grinding his cock against it, his peachy bum rising and falling slightly, like a powerful engine slowly ticking over.

'You may end up with pre-come on your duvet,' he said apologetically. 'Hope you're OK with that.'

'Fine with it,' I said. By now I was kneeling beside him on the bed, legs a little way apart, rolling on the condom. 'With any luck you'll also come on it.'

Simon giggled into the pillow, still rubbing his dick against the cover, while I straddled him. I lubed a finger and inserted it into him, testing how relaxed he was. It made me think of Simon's line of work for a moment…

Inserting a rectal thermometer.

He relaxed quickly. 'Can you raise your arse a bit?' I asked him, and he did so. Then I pushed my longish but not frighteningly thick dick, sheathed and lubed, inside him.

He grunted a few times as I made my inward journey. I slowed up each time and continued on more gently. Then, when I was all the way in I started to rod him slowly...

I took it gently. After all, we were in no hurry. My thrustings repeatedly shoved his cock against the bed-cover. To my surprise, and perhaps to his also, he suddenly called out, 'Oh hey, I'm coming!' And I felt his body buck, then buckle beneath me.

That got me suddenly even more excited and I speeded up my action. A moment later it was my turn to call out that I was coming. I squirted deep inside him, filling my condom.

We lay where we were, locked together, for a minute or more while we recovered. Then I rolled off him, twisting my dick out of him as I did so. Now lying beside him I said, 'Roll back. Let me see what you've done to my duvet.'

Obediently he moved onto his side. His cock-tip still drooled sticky streamers. He'd created a big glossy lake beneath him, about six inches in diameter. On his tummy was painted a glistening mirror image of it.

*

Lunch was quiche and salad. A glass of chilled white wine to go with it. I took him for a short drive after that. Although he'd known the area well since childhood he didn't know the particular road I lived on. You couldn't see the sea from my house but a two-mile drive brought you rather surprisingly in sight of it. I showed the view to Simon – the broad bay, the jutting headland with its lighthouse, and he was suitably impressed by it. We drove back the way we'd come. That is, with our hands crossed above the gear-stick and stroking each other's thighs gently.

When we got back to my place, there was Tim, about to get into his car on the driveway. He turned and looked at us for a second. No smile. No light in his eyes. He turned away again without acknowledging us and unlocked his Mini. By the time we'd got out of my car he'd driven off in it with a noisy stab to the accelerator.

Neither Simon or I commented on Tim's behaviour. We gave each other a look, though.

'Time for a shower before you go?' I asked Simon.

'Yes,' he said, and grinned at me. We both knew what showering together would involve. And it did, of course. We both came a second time, standing together under the running water. Then we had a brief lie-down and cool-off on the bed together. We were all the more relaxed and at ease for the fact that Tim wasn't around to brood on whatever he might imagine that Simon and I were doing together.

Eventually it was time for Simon to get up and drive back to his parents' house in Westbourne. We agreed we'd meet again soon. Tim hadn't returned home when I went out on the driveway to wave goodbye to Simon. I was quite glad of that. I resolved to give Tim no further thought that evening.

*

Not thinking about Tim was easier said than done. He had preoccupied my waking thoughts ever since Thursday, and having a visit from, and sex with, Simon – lovely though that was – had made no difference to that. Now his blanking of us and driving away from us like a bat out of hell had made it even more difficult to get the boy out of my thoughts. His car came back in the early evening – supper time with dad, I thought – and I was reassured to know he was back. I hadn't really thought he had driven over the nearest cliff (it was only three miles distant) but even so…

I was determined, though, to draw no conclusions about Tim's behaviour until I'd spoken to him next. One deduction I might have made was that the boy had a crush on me and that Simon's arrival on the scene had put his nose out of joint. People in that situation often do behave the way Tim had. But that interpretation was altogether too flattering to myself, too absurd, and I refused to entertain it.

By the end of the evening, though, I found I couldn't

wait to get to the bottom of it. After a lot of almost emailing him and then not doing so I finally typed the address Tim had given me and sent him a message. *Is everything OK with you, Tim? With very best wishes, Will.* When I went to bed I could see from my side window that his bedroom light was on (so was his father's) which meant that he was probably on his computer, but no reply to my email had come. I went to bed.

*

I saw Tim the next day, Sunday. I made a point of tidying things up at the front of the house, to be in hailing distance of him if or when he materialised on the driveway. His father materialised more than once. 'You're busy,' he said. Then, 'Up for a drink tonight?' To which I said yes of course. We arranged it for his place. I was wondering whether Tim would show his face while I was chewing the fat with his father in his own house when he suddenly appeared from the front door and headed towards his Mini.

'Hi, Tim,' I called brightly. He neither returned my greeting nor looked in my direction. I made a point of not watching him as he drove off. Inwardly I heaved a sigh. The boy certainly knew how to sulk.

That evening I chatted with Michael as per normal. Tim didn't make an appearance, though occasionally we heard his footsteps above our heads as he moved about his bedroom. 'How's Tim?' I asked Michael casually – or pretend-casually. And Michael told me happily and innocently about his son's developing plans for university in the autumn, and his occasional worries about impending exams and the results of them.

'He doesn't need to worry,' I said. 'He's one of the brightest kids on the block.'

'You know that and I know that,' Michael said. 'But try telling him that.'

'Perhaps I will,' I said, smiling. 'Next time I find the two of us having a chat.'

'No time like the present, I suppose,' said Michael. 'I'll call him down. See if he'll join us in a glass.'

Michael got up and went out into the hall. I heard him call Tim from there. I heard no answering voice, or sound of opening door. I heard his father go upstairs. He disappeared from my radar for a bit. Then he was back in the room with me again.

'No,' he said. 'He's deep in one of his computer games, involving people from all over the world. You know how it is.'

'Perfectly understandable,' I said. 'Kid of his age. Has his own friends to drink with when he wants to. No reason he'd want to sit about sipping wine with old codgers like us.'

'All the same,' said Michael. 'Sometimes there's the matter of being polite. We all have to bite the bullet and spend time with people we don't particularly want to be with for the sake of that.'

'He'll learn,' I said. 'All part of growing up.' And that was the end of our conversation about Tim as far as that evening went. We talked of other things and got slightly and pleasantly tipsy, and I wished that the evening didn't have to end with me saying goodnight in the hallway and a one-way street of a kiss.

When I got home – some thirty seconds later – I did something one should never do. I fired off a late-night, half drunken, email. Pressed send, rather than wait, as one always should, to re-read it in the cold light of morning.

Tim, why are you blanking me? I know we agreed that we wouldn't go on with our last conversation unless you particularly wanted to. But I don't think that's the same as agreeing that you would then ignore my existence. Just say hallo sometime. There are no strings attached to that. All the very best. And with love. Will xx

Needless to say, no reply came to that. Not that night, nor the next morning, when I checked my in-box just before going to work. Tim had left for college by that time. Yes, of course I looked to check.

*

I finished work at four that afternoon. Took my protective and antiseptic clothing off and walked out through the patients' waiting area. By that time of the afternoon it was usually empty. But today one young man sat alone among the rows of plastic seats. Very forlorn he looked, sitting there at this time of day. It took me only half a second to realise who I was looking at. 'Tim,' I said, 'what are you doing here?' I added quickly, 'Not that I'm not pleased to see you.'

He looked up at me with a mask-like face. I knew that look. Had he tried to smile at me something else would have happened. I would have to tread carefully. I didn't want him to lose his cool in front of me; didn't want him to be embarrassed.

'I wanted to see you,' he said.

I couldn't help smiling. Perhaps I would be the one to break down and lose it. 'Good,' I said. Then, 'Where's your car?'

'I left it at college,' he said. 'I got the bus up.'

'Oh right,' I said calmly, while my mind whirled, trying to deal with the possible and the imaginable implications of that. 'Mine's in the staff car-park. Shall we walk out that way?'

He could have said no to that but he didn't. Instead he accompanied me meekly, walking through the maze of corridors alongside me. I didn't speak. He had come looking for me. If there was to be a conversation it was up to him to start it.

Not till we'd left the hospital building and we were out in the sunshine among the crowded car-parks did he open his mouth. 'You care about me,' he said.

'Yes,' I said. I had to leave it at that.

'I didn't realise till you sent that email last night. The way you ended it…'

'Yes,' I said.

'But you had sex with Simon on Saturday.' The alliteration made it sound like the title of a book.

'Yes, I did,' I said. Good God! Did he feel I'd been unfaithful to him or something? I would have to tread very carefully with this. I took a deep breath. We had nearly reached the car. 'I'm very fond of you, Tim,' I said. 'Fonder than I ought to be. Does that make sense?'

'Yes,' he said, in a voice no bigger than a breath.

We'd reached the car. We stopped. 'Will you get in with me?' I asked.

'Yes,' he said. We separated just enough to walk round to opposite sides of the car. I clicked my key-fob to unlock it and we both got into it.

I didn't start the engine at once. We sat together, side by side, not touching each other, in the front seats.

'Were you upset by Simon coming round?' I asked.

'Perhaps,' he said.

'I knew I was fond of you,' I said. 'That I cared for you, as you put it. I didn't dare to think… Well, you know what I didn't dare to think.'

'That I cared for you?'

'If I had thought that I would have been more diplomatic.'

'By having it off with Simon somewhere else?'

I ignored that. 'If I had known that, instead of just thinking it, I wouldn't have had it off with Simon at all.'

At that moment I felt the tentative alighting of a hand on my thigh, soft as the landing of a moth.

'Shall I drive us home?' I asked. 'Or do you want to go somewhere else.'

'Home,' he said. 'Only – could we stop off somewhere on the way for a drink?'

EIGHT

Pure joy was what I experienced at that moment when he touched my thigh. It came dizzyingly like the quick high of a first pull on a cigarette after years of abstinence. But equally instantaneously came awareness of the difficulties that the new situation would create for itself if it was allowed to develop. We couldn't now simply drive to the pub in our home village and walk in together. Well, we could. But it would cause a frisson. People would talk. Michael's farmer customers gathered there. 'Saw your son in the Green Dragon the other day,' they would delight in telling him within the first minute of their next encounter with him. 'With your neighbour Will.' They wouldn't be so impolite as to tell Michael what inference they had drawn from our coming into the pub together for a heart to heart talk over a quick half-pint. But Michael would know what they had made of it. And then he would be left to think about what he was going to have to make of it.

'Can't really go to the Green Dragon,' I told Tim as we drove off. I didn't need to explain. He agreed with a sage nod of his head. He'd grown up in the village. He knew what villages were like.

We turned off the road and took a byway to another village. The people in the pub there would speculate, after we'd left, about the nature of our relationship ('Them two don't look much like father and son,') but at least they wouldn't know who they were speculating about. There would be nowhere for the news to travel to, and our visit would quickly be forgotten about.

The Queen's Head was a lovely oak-beamed Elizabethan inn, with a cosy interior that was warmed and brightened by a log fire in a huge hearth. We settled for a half of bitter each. I was glad that Tim was OK with that. I would need to be careful not to return Tim to his father in any kind of a state. It would be a difficult enough return anyway. Tim was going to have to explain where his car had got to, how come I'd been on hand to give him a lift home, the circumstances in which we'd met... And why we'd gone together to a pub...

Michael and I rarely went to the Green Dragon together. For the same reason that his son and I hadn't gone there tonight. People talked. Whenever Michael and I had gone into the Dragon we always heard afterwards what people had said. 'Is that Will's new boyfriend?' 'Handsome bloke.' 'Pair of handsome blokes.' 'No, that's his neighbour.' 'Yes. Know him well. Didn't know he was like that, though.' 'He's not like that. He's got a woman up Marlpits way.' 'No smoke without fire, though...' Et cetera.

I was sitting across a polished oak pub table from, and gazing into the blue eyes of, the loveliest teenager I'd ever had the honour to be in company with. Objectively speaking perhaps he wasn't the most beautiful teenager I'd ever seen. I'd seen handsomer guys in movies and in porn videos. But only a few. It was beside the point anyway. Tim was the loveliest teenager in the world for me, quite obviously, because he was the only one I had. I could imagine Michael having the same feeling. For Michael Tim was the loveliest guy in the world. Because he was his son. Now I thought I shared that emotion. Tim was the loveliest guy in the world – flashing blue eyes across the table – because he was my guy. I thought about my friendship with Michael. Glumly I saw a potential conflict of interests.

I was sitting across a table from the most gorgeous man I'd ever met, sharing the log-fired ambience of a beautiful cosy pub… And I couldn't think of a word to say.

Happily, Tim was more inspired than I was. 'What does it feel like when you get fucked?' he asked.

Sometimes in this situation it's good to have something practical to talk about.

'It depends,' I said. 'Depends who you are, and who the other person is.'

'Could you elaborate?' he asked, like one of his college teachers, I guessed. Then he twinkled his blue eyes at me.

'I think it helps if you're a reasonably good fit in terms of size. That's to state the obvious. If you're a small person you wouldn't want anything too enormous barging its way into you. There may be a few people who relish the pain of that – whatever floats your boat – but I'm not one of them. The other main thing is, some people's prostate glands are positioned in such a way that getting fucked brings them off without anyone or anything having to touch their penis. That's a physiological thing: nothing to do with being gay or straight.'

'Does getting fucked bring you off?' Tim asked. An edge of excitement had crept into his voice, overtaking his earlier clinical detachment.

'Sadly not,' I said. 'At least it's never happened yet. Perhaps it would take a specially shaped cock such as I've never had the pleasure to meet yet. For me, getting fucked is mildly pleasurable, provided I like the person who's doing it to me. Part of being together and belonging together. But it never gives me quite the same pleasure as I get from fucking somebody else.'

I saw a tense look come over his face, which made me realise I needed to say something else. 'Not all gay people fuck each other or like being fucked. There's plenty of fun to be had doing other stuff – wanking each other, sucking each other's cocks. There's no obligation for a gay guy to fuck or be fucked. There's no obligation actually to do any of the physical stuff if you don't want to do it.'

'I want to do some of it,' Tim said. 'I've done some of it. It's just that I'm not sure about being fucked.'

'Neither was I at your age,' I said. 'I didn't fuck anyone or get fucked by anyone till I was twenty. But I'd had plenty of fun before that, doing the other stuff.'

We exchanged very cosy smiles at that point. I think we were both amazed that we'd had that conversation in the ambience of a village pub, with people sitting around us. True, we'd kept our voices prudently quiet.

I still wasn't quite sure, though, whether Tim actually wanted sex – any sort of sex – with me at all. All we'd ascertained so far was that he didn't want me having sex with anybody else. If his ambitions as far as I was concerned went only as far as having me as a friend he could talk to… well, then that requirement would have been a rather big ask.

We were now sitting facing each other in silence. Neither of us knew what was going to happen next, or who would speak first. As it turned out I spoke first. 'I'm not sure what's going to happen now. Between us, I mean. I'm not sure what you want or expect. Maybe you don't either. So I'll be brave for a moment. Or bold, or foolhardy … and tell you that I think you're lovely.'

'I think you're lovely too,' he said.

You can't do, I thought. *I'm twenty years your senior.* But I didn't tell him that. You don't look a gift horse in the mouth. Even if you think the giver has come to the wrong address.

'So,' I said, thinking as I went. 'Do you want us to meet?'

'Yes,' he said.

'It may be difficult,' I cautioned. 'I know we live next door, but your father's my closest friend.'

'Easter holidays start in two days,' he said calmly. 'I'll be home all day while dad's at work.'

'My God, you are a cool cucumber,' I said.

He laughed. 'I've never been called a cucumber before,' he said.

'Cool though,' I said. 'You must have been called that.'

He shuffled on his seat. 'Maybe once or twice.'

'You may be free all day for a couple of weeks,' I said, aware that I was about to pour cold water on his plans, 'but I still have to go to work.'

'Sometimes you get time off midweek, though…' he went on hopefully.

'I'll see what I can do,' I said. 'We'll find a way somehow. Find times to meet…'

'We must,' he said. He sounded very sure about that.

'We'd better drink up,' I said. 'It's time I took you back. Your dad'll wonder…'

'I'll call him,' Tim said. 'Tell him I'm on my way. Then we can use the time in the car going back to make something up.'

I sighed. 'Your call,' I said. As we stood up to go he got his phone out.

We restrained ourselves as we crossed the pub car-park. Walked side by side, not touching. Tim very coolly told his father that I was bringing him home and that he'd be back in ten minutes. He put the phone back in his pocket and turned to me. 'I'll tell him you just happened to be driving past the college at the moment I was walking out. And that you'll take me back in the morning.' He thought for a second. 'You will, won't you?'

'Of course,' I said. 'But your story makes me look like… Oh, never mind. Can't be helped.'

'Well, if you can think of a better story…'

'I can't,' I said. 'I'll just have to be ready with some explanation of what I was doing down by the college if he asks.' Oh dear. Here I was, planning to lie to my dearest friend, the man who – since Aidan's death – I loved best on the whole planet.

We got into the car. And then it was as if a dam had burst. Though it was daylight and anyone could have seen us through the car windows we were all over each other at once. Arms around each other, feeling shoulders, chests. Pinching nipples. Eventually diving towards crotches, truffling out erections from behind prised-open zips. Kissing with open mouths.

I felt the wonder of his hot cock-shaft in my hand before I saw it. And the same went for Tim. 'You're big,' he said.

'And you're beautiful,'   I said.

I came to my senses. 'We must put them away,' I said. 'I've got to drive you home. We'll be arrested if we go on like this.'

'Yep,' said Tim, a mixture of common sense and reluctance. He stuffed his hard penis back inside his jeans – with some difficulty – and zipped himself up; then I followed suit. I started the engine, we fastened our seat-belts and I drove off.

As we went along we rested a hand on each other's thigh. Tim's touch was no longer timid and tentative but firm and confident. Mine too. We even unzipped each other at one point, driving through a mile of deep countryside between two villages, and had another feel of each other. 'Oh God,' said Tim, 'you're making me so wet.' I thought he might come among my exploring fingers but by the time we reached the outskirts of our home village and we had to zip up again he still hadn't. I foresaw him running up to his bedroom within a minute of arriving home and finishing himself off in a quick violent explosion of semen. I foresaw myself doing the same thing.

'We can keep in touch by email and text over the next few days,' he said. 'I'm sorry I didn't answer your last one.'

'That's quite all right,' I said. 'I completely understand that. And yes, we'll keep in touch that way.' By now we were in sight of our two houses. 'But I'm seeing you tomorrow morning,' I reminded him. 'Taking you back to college – unless your father sees through your story and vetoes it. Eight o'clock out on the driveway on the dot. Don't be late.'

We were just pulling up when Tim asked suddenly, 'Do you still masturbate? I know dad does.'

'Do I still…? Of course I do. Everybody does. And I certainly will tonight. You too, I guess.'

'You bet,' he said, and laughed. 'Probably within the next ten minutes.'

'Same here,' I said. I switched the engine off. Tim un-clicked his seat-belt. He paused a second before opening the door. 'Email later,' he said. 'And see you in the morning, eight o'clock.'

'Right,' I said to his departing back. By the time I got out of the car he had disappeared from sight.

I hoped that when he explained things to his father Michael wouldn't see too easily through his fragile fib. If he did – if he began to suspect that I was getting sexually involved with his son the consequences would be terrible for all of us.

I let myself into my house, went straight up to my bedroom, and threw myself onto the bed.

*

I checked my inbox hourly that evening. There was nothing from Tim till ten o'clock. Then there was. *Hi Will,* he'd written. *Have you done it yet?*

Yes, I emailed back. *Of course I have. What about you?*

Ditto, he wrote back at once. *Twice.*

I wrote back mock-sternly. *8 o'clock tomorrow, remember. Time you were in bed.*

I am in bed, he replied a few minutes later. *Writing this on my phone. Playing with myself.*

Go to sleep, I wrote.

Nite-nite, he wrote back.

He was out on the driveway at eight on the dot. We got into my car together. Michael had already left for work. 'Was your dad all right about things?' I asked.

'Slightly puzzled, perhaps,' he said. 'But not worried about anything. No suspicions about us.'

A few minutes later we drew up outside the college. A few young people peered in at us. 'Have a good day, darling,' I said. 'We'll find a way to meet in private soon… Oh shit!' I said, recollecting myself. 'I just called you darling. I'm sorry. I shouldn't have done that.'

'It's OK,' he said brightly, un-doing his seat-belt. 'Actually it's nice. No-one's called me darling since Mummy died.' Then he'd opened the door and was out of it. A moment later he was invisible among the crowd around the college gates.

NINE

Tim told me in an email that he would be at home all day on Friday while his father was out at work. If I could get the day off… He would come round to my front door in the morning, after his father had left. Of course I phoned the hospital immediately and begged to take Friday off.

Before Friday came round I had my weekly evening with Michael. At my house this time. The experience seemed a bit surreal in the circumstances. I watched Michael stretch his elegant long legs across the carpet in front of him as he sat in his accustomed armchair opposite mine and I tried to stop myself glancing sideways at the sofa on which his son and I had had our first kiss and cuddle a fortnight earlier.

'How's Tim?' I asked about half an hour (and a glass of wine) later. I wasn't sure whether I was being reckless by bringing up the subject of my friend's son, or whether I would have attracted more suspicion if I'd gone all evening without mentioning someone I'd driven home from college and taken back there again just two days earlier.

'He's fine,' Michael said. 'Actually more cheerful than usual these last few days. Maybe there's a girl on the scene.' He rearranged his legs and took a sip from his glass. 'It's not something I'm going to ask.'

'No,' I said carefully and took a sip of wine myself.

'Of course.'

'Thanks for bringing him home the other day, by the way. And taking him back. That's cut his petrol bill a bit. How did you come to be going past the college, though?'

I was ready for this. 'I'd been to Argos. Got myself a new cheapo iron. I always come back that way on the rare occasions I go to Argos. I happened to see Tim in the road.' Michael wouldn't want to see the new iron, would he? Assuming it would have cost about five quid. It would hardly be worth getting out of a cosy armchair for and making a trip to the kitchen. I hoped he wouldn't anyway, because there wasn't one. Luckily he did not.

There. I'd done it. Lied deliberately to my best friend. To the man I loved. Or to one of them. I didn't feel good about that. I took a large slurp from my wineglass.

'He's getting quite excited about uni,' Michael went on. Quietly I breathed my relief. 'Hopes he'll end up at Brighton now. Last week it was Leeds he wanted most.' We shared a laugh over the fickle enthusiasms of those who were younger than us.

'Brighton's not too far away, though,' I said. We looked at each other in silence. We were sharing the thought that Tim's departure to university in the autumn would leave Michael alone in his house. Alone and lonely as I was. And I too would be bereft by Tim's leaving the village. Only I wouldn't be able to tell Michael that.

I changed the subject. Easter was late this year. We were already approaching the middle of April. 'Have you heard the cuckoo yet?'

Michael smiled. 'Yes. Today for the first time. Down by the river near Conster.' Conster was one of the farms he supplied with stocks and equipment.

*

The cuckoo called nearer home on Friday morning. I heard it from among the trees across the road as soon as I awoke. Sign of a new spring – in my heart too perhaps? – it seemed like a good omen for this unprecedented day. For all my experience of love and sex and lust I really had no idea how this day – the day I was going to spend in the company of my best friend's son – was going to turn out.

Like someone who'd been thinking about how early in the morning he could dare to make an important phone-call Tim rang my doorbell on the dot of nine o'clock.

He looked gorgeous. Tight, clean-on blue jeans, impeccable white trainers and socks. A crisply ironed white shirt, undone to the third button. Vanilla-strawberry ice cream chest showing bravely-coyly underneath. Somebody had ironed that shirt. He himself? His doting father? I tried to stop thinking about that before it hurt too deep. 'Come in,' I said.

'Thanks,' he said.

'You look gorgeous,' I said,

'Thanks,' he said.

He threw his arms around me there and then in the hallway, standing on the doormat: the same place where I so often threw my arms around his dad. 'What do you want to do?' I asked between his kisses. I was too awestruck to think straight. 'Would you like to come upstairs?'

'Yes please,' he said.

We climbed the stairs together. He stood in my bedroom for the first time, looking around him, of course, even as he focused his attention on me. I didn't make any move to undress him. Instead I undressed myself. He watched till I was nearly naked, my cock standing to attention in front of him, then without touching me he solemnly divested himself.

I don't have the power to describe how lovely he looked. His legs were lightly striated with dark hairs, pleasingly modelled, not over muscular, in shape. His upper half was almost hairless, except for the bushes of his armpits and a treasure trail that started from nowhere, just below his navel, and ran down to ... well, you know where.

'I'm sorry I'm not as big as you,' he said.

'Sorry?' I said. I was too overcome to laugh. Couldn't manage even a friendly comradely laugh. I was too close to tears for that. 'You're   beautiful,' I said.

We moved in to each other. We held each other tight, exchanging the warmth of our bellies, chests and arms – inhaling the scent of each other – and feeding each other and ourselves with all of that.

'I love you,' Tim said.

I closed my eyes. I wasn't sure how to deal with this. I'd been half expecting it. I knew what it was like to fall for someone older than myself. Even so… But there was only one possible answer to the avowal at this moment. 'I love you too,' I said.

I wasn't sure what to do now. 'Shall we lie down?' I said. It seemed the safest bet.

I lay flat on my back and he lay on top of me, rubbing his cock against my belly, and in the process rubbing my cock against his.

'Oh no,' he said. 'I'm going to come.'

'Go for it,' I said.

He gave a couple of small thrusts with his hips and, though I couldn't see it, I felt his cock pulse repeatedly and his warm milk pour out. He continued to lie on top of me and I felt him gradually relax. Neither of us spoke. I stroked his hair and his back. I got the impression he'd have purred if he'd been a cat.

After a few minutes he rolled off me. I saw him peer at my belly, inspecting his results. I said, 'That was nice. Want to do me now?' We were both still very stiff.

'Do you mind if I just watch you do yourself?' he asked. 'This time.'

'That's fine,' I said. With the blade of my hand I gathered up what I could of his semen pool and used it to lube myself. He hadn't come as copiously as Simon usually did, but Simon's output was exceptional, prodigious. But where Tim was concerned I had no complaints.

Then I went at it. Tim lay on his side next to me, watching intently. 'This won't take long,' I said.

Tim snuggled in close to me and started to finger my chest. 'You'll make me go,' I said. 'Come, I mean. Come or go, same difference.'

'Go for it,' Tim said.

And I did. I shot suddenly.

'Oh fuck,' said Tim when my spurting had finished and we'd both calmed down a bit. 'That was amazing.'

'I know,' I said. 'I amazed myself. I don't normally go like that. That was the effect you had.'

'Oh wow,' said Tim. He sounded a bit shaken by the compliment.

I handed Tim a towel from the locker. 'Prepared for everything,' I said, and Tim laughed. Then he mopped us both up.

'We can shower later,' I said. 'In the meantime, it's a

lovely morning. Would you like to go for a walk?'

'Round here?' he said.

'Why not?'

He had no answer to that, so out we went.

*

We headed down the main road for a bit. If any of our neighbours were looking out and saw us... Well, they could think what they liked. Presumably Tim had the same thought, if he thought about it at all. At any rate he made no comment on the possibility of our being spotted, nor did he make any effort to conceal himself. He was out and about in my company. He didn't seem ashamed or embarrassed by the fact.

'I hardly ever walk around here,' he said.

'I know,' I said. 'I've noticed that. It's really nice to cut down the lane on the left. Know that? Down to the stream, up through the woods the other side to Bullmarsh.'

'That sounds like a hell of a long walk,' he said.

'Too far? We've got all day. We could have a pub lunch in Bullmarsh. (You're not known in the pub there, are you?) Maybe have a lie down and a cuddle in a field on the way back...?'

'OK,' he said. He turned to me and grinned broadly. 'I'm up for it.' Then he heard something. 'Oh hey,' he said. 'There's a cuckoo. First one I've heard this year.'

'I heard it this morning,' I said. 'But your dad has the edge. He heard it two days ago down at Conster.'

'He never told me that,' Tim said.

'Perhaps he didn't think you'd be interested,' I said. 'He only told me because I asked him.'

'Hmm,' he said. 'I've often wondered what the two of you tall about each week.' His blue eyes twinkled humorously. 'Bloody garden birds. Must be riveting.'

'Actually,' I said, 'we talk about you quite a lot.' We'd reached the lane that dived down to the stream a mile away. We turned down into the lane and I gave his ear a tweak.

The sun shone across the valley. It lit the patchwork of fields and copses, picking out the thin green hues of April where it could, and the purple haze of the woods – bud-cases ready to burst in millions – where it could not.

We stopped by the stream and looked over the bridge. 'Can we see fish?' Tim asked.

'I doubt it. Too much clay here. You can't see through the water. You need chalk country and clear streams to actually see fish.'

'You know a lot about nature,' Tim said.

'Only a bit,' I said.

We went on up the hill on the other side. Here the lane was very steep. My heart was pounding by the time we reached the top. That was due in part to the effort of the climb – but only in part.

At the top of the hill the lane entered a wood. But the wood was patchy, full of clearings made by loggers. At one point there was a clear view back down the way we'd come, and to the high ground opposite. Tim said suddenly, 'Look at that!' I followed his pointing finger. A gap in the hillside some miles distant framed a view of a container ship. 'I didn't know you could see the sea from here,' he said.

'Neither did I,' I said. 'It must be exceptionally clear today.'

'Pretty exceptional day all round,' Tim said. He added, 'So far at any rate.'

'I think we can keep it that way,' I said. I drew him towards me and we kissed. In plain sight of anyone on that container ship eight miles away who might be looking our way through a telescope.

A few minutes later we came to the gateway of a track that led deep into the woods. I stopped. 'I could show you something if you liked,' I said. 'But I'd understand if you didn't want to. You might find it gruesome or disturbing.'

'Try me,' Tim said.

'It's the place where I scattered Aidan's ashes two

years ago.' At once I regretted saying that. 'Sorry,' I said. 'That wasn't appropriate. Not for a morning like this.'

I felt Tim's fingers steal in amongst mine. 'Don't be sorry,' he said. 'It's important for you. Which means it's important for me too. Take me there. Show me.'

We walked up the track through the still wintry trees, some just breaking bud, others still sheathed. It was warm, though, and the grass and the brambles were already greening up. We came to a fork in the track. It formed a small clearing that was full of primroses. In the middle was a simple wooden seat. Just a plank on two supports set in the earth. 'Aidan and I used to sit here,' I said. 'In the weeks before he died.'

'Can we sit here?' Tim asked.

'Of course,' I said. I felt honoured – and I felt that Aidan was being honoured – by that request.

We sat down side by side. We didn't touch or kiss. 'He was older than you,' said Tim.

'Yes,' I said. 'By quite a bit.'

'And it was cancer he died of.'

'Yes,' I said. 'It came on suddenly and was mercifully quick. He died one night in his sleep.'

'I should have got to know him better,' Tim said.

'You were just a kid. You're getting to know me

better now, anyway. I guess I'm standing in, these days, for both of us.'

'Hmm,' he said, in a tone of interest. It seemed he appreciated the thought. 'And now he's...'

'All around us,' I said. 'I scattered his ashes all around this spot. He's part of the grass and the primroses.'

'That's what I thought,' Tim said. 'I like the idea of that. The primroses are beautiful. I remember the day you scattered his ashes. You came back and took dad out for a drink.'

'That's right,' I said. 'We went to the Green Dragon and he bought me a pint. Then I bought him one back.'

'Dad likes you a lot,' Tim said. Then, 'Would it be OK for me to give you a kiss? I mean, at this spot, on this bench.'

'I'd like that very much,' I said. We leaned in towards each other and kissed rather soberly. Then I felt him groping at my trousers in search of my cock. He gave it a squeeze through the fabric. I returned the compliment. But we left it at that. We didn't take them out, and neither of us was stiff. 'Come on,' I said. 'We've paid our respects.' We stood up and walked away from the sunlit clearing, towards the gate and the lane, while birds sang their spring songs in the trees above our heads.

TEN

We walked right to the end of the lane, where it opened out into the main road that ran through Bullmarsh. We turned towards the pub. I felt I was eighteen again. I suppose that was how Tim must have felt too. Because that was the age he actually was.

'You make me feel very young again,' I said.

'And you make me feel like a very small kid.'

Hmm. Whatever my fond imaginings, there would always remain twenty years between us.

It was only a little after twelve o'clock but we went straight into the pub. I asked him what he wanted. Bitter, he said. I'd drunk a half pint with him once. Never a full pint. I gave him the choice in an even-handed tone of voice. I didn't want to seem penny-pinching. Neither did I want to get him drunk. He chose a pint. We both chose a pint. And a toasted sandwich of ham and cheese. 'The walk back should sober us up,' Tim said. He was right. We'd walked over three miles to get here. It would be the same on the way back.

'You'll need to get your breath sorted before your dad gets back from work,' I cautioned him.

'Yes,' he said. 'And I'm cooking supper tonight.'

'Are you?' That surprised me a bit. I imagined Tim spent all his time at his computer desk. I hadn't visualised him in the role of kitchen sprite.

'Yeah. Sometimes, if I'm at home all day and he's out at work… Well, it's only fair.'

If I hadn't fallen for Tim already I would have done at that moment. What a lovely son he must be to have… 'What are you cooking tonight?' I asked.

'Pasta with tuna and peppers,' he said. It sounded good. I decided not to go on down this conversational avenue, enticing though it was. It would look as if I was angling for an invite.

The pub wasn't very busy yet. There were no familiar faces in it and I was glad about that. I didn't ask Tim if he recognised anyone, but from the nonchalant way that he took the nearby faces in and then looked calmly away again I guessed he didn't.

We didn't linger very long over our light lunch. There were things I wanted to do with Tim, things I wanted to say to him, that couldn't be done, couldn't be said, in a public place.

Once we were back in the lane, out of sight of the main road and the houses on it, Tim couldn't keep his hands off me, which was very nice. The one pint dose had been just about right, I thought. After about half a mile Tim stopped by a field gate. 'I need a piss,' he said, and turned away from me towards the gate.

'You don't need to be shy with me,' I said. 'I like looking at your cock.'

'What? Even when I'm pissing through it?'

'Even when you're pissing through it,' I said. I'd nearly said, 'Especially when you're pissing through it,' but decided against that. At any rate he lost his shyness and turned back towards me as he got his cock out. With my attention as well as his own upon it, plus his pressing need to urinate, it was already beginning to thicken up. He started to piss, in fits and spurts.

To help things along a bit I got my own out and followed his example. We stood facing each other, our streams occasionally intercepting each other with a sparkling clash, and we alternately looked up coyly, bashfully, at each other's eyes and giggled, and looked down at each other's cocks. It hardly needs to be said that by the time we'd emptied ourselves out we were both completely stiff.

Once I was sure it was safe to do so without getting my hand wetted by a final surprise squirt I reached for his hard dick and held it as though claiming a prize I'd been awarded. And he grabbed mine. He scooped my balls out. I scooped his out. Tentatively we began to slide our hands back and forth on each other's shafts.

'A car might come past,' I said after a moment. 'I think we need to get over the gate and behind the hedge.'

There was a first time for everything, it seemed. I'd never before climbed a gate with a boner and my bollocks sticking out of my trousers, in company with a boy who was in the identical state. But that was what we did. The gate was made of tubular metal and was rusty. We had to be careful not to bang our cocks on the bars as we went over it.

The field had had sheep in it, evidently, for the grass was bitten short, but it was now empty, and the sheep droppings dried to dust and innocuous. I manoeuvred Tim out of the sightline from the gate, to a place behind the hedge but not too close to its roots – where adders might have lurked. 'Lie down,' I said.

Looking around at the grass most carefully we got down onto it. Our cocks were still poking out of our open flies. I undid the stud at Tim's waistband and pulled his jeans and underpants down to his knees in one movement. He helped me by taking the weight off his bottom with feet and elbows as I slid his leg-wear down his thighs.

He pulled his shirt up till I could see his navel, then he turned his attention to me and carried out the reciprocal process. I gave his dick a reassuring squeeze. To my delight Tim reached out towards mine, clasped it, first gently then more firmly. 'Yours is massive,' he said. 'Much bigger than Tyler's.'

'That's nice to hear,' I said. 'Though I'm twice as old as Tyler. I'm sure his is lovely too though.'

Yes,' said Tim. 'It is.' We both left it at that.

Side by side we lay on our backs, looking up at the cloud-flecked blue sky and at each other – into each other's eyes from time to time, and interestedly at each other's cocks. Masturbating each other like two old friends who'd been doing this for years. As I used to do with Aidan in fact.

'I'll come too soon again,' Tim said.

'It doesn't matter if you do,' I said. 'We can do it again in the shower when we get back. We've got all afternoon still.'

By now he was jerking his legs about. I thought – for the first time ever – that having your knees shackled together by half-dropped trousers while you worked towards a climax was actually rather like an elementary form of bondage. Not that I had experience of the more advanced sort… I rolled half towards him and with my spare hand tickled his clenched balls. 'Oh shit, I'm coming,' he said. 'I want to do it on you again,' he added urgently, and rolled himself towards me a bit.

'Feel free,' I said, and speeded up my stroke.

This time I saw it. It went all over my shirt.

'Sorry,' he said a minute later. 'I didn't mean to wet your shirt.'

'It's fine,' I said. 'I couldn't be happier about that in fact. But in the meantime are you going to finish me off or do you want me to do that myself?'

'I'll finish you,' he said. 'It's only fair.' Like cooking his father's supper sometimes, I thought.

'What are you smiling at?' he asked as he resumed his

stroking of my cock.

'Nothing. Just you,' I said. 'And you won't have to work away for ages. Don't worry. I'm nearly ready to come, I think.' And half a minute later I did, turning a little further towards him and spurting most of my load against his belly where his wispy treasure trail met his see-through pubic bush. 'How's that?' I said. But he took the moment more seriously. He pressed himself wetly against me, put both arms round my neck, nuzzled his head into my collar and held me tightly, silently, as if he never wanted to let go. I was humbled, even shaken, by that. I hugged him tightly back and stroked his head. I think he might have been crying. I didn't ask.

*

We talked lightly about sex as we continued our walk back. 'You asked me in an email a week or so back if I still wanked,' I said. 'You added that you knew your father did. How did you know that? I mean, I've always assumed he does, because everybody does – all men anyway – but how do *you* know that?'

Tim sniggered. 'I caught him once.'

'Go on,' I said.

'He came in from work once and for some reason he didn't think I was in the house. He took a shower, leaving the bathroom door open. I happened to go past and I saw him through the glass.'

'Giving himself one, standing up...?' I was getting a

little excited by this.

'It was a bit misty and difficult to see, but yes. He'd lathered himself up and was standing there doing it…'

'Did he see you?'

'I don't think so. I crept away very quietly. A few minutes later I made a point of making a clatter in another part of the house so he'd know I was around the place. If he did see me … he never mentioned it.'

'I don't suppose he would have done,' I said. I just managed to keep a straight face. I shouldn't really have asked the next thing – it was rather taking advantage – but I did. 'Has he got a big cock?'

'That was the only time I've ever seen it stiff. I've seen it at other times, though, when it's soft. It's longer than yours – quite a bit longer. Not much thicker, though. And his balls aren't big like yours are. They're small, like mine are.'

'Nothing wrong with that,' I said. 'Your balls are lovely.' I just managed not to add that I thought his father's balls would be lovely too. I found myself longing all over again to get my hands on Michael. To fondle his small balls while I performed a sword-swallowing act on his dick… I didn't tell Tim I was thinking this. Though he may well have guessed.

'Like us he's uncircumcised,' Tim said.

'I did know that,' I said smugly.'

'How do you know that?'

Even more smugly I said, 'He's told me that.' I was still glowing with the warmth of Tim's phrase – *like us*.

We walked back through the woods. Past the gate that led to Aidan's last resting place among the primroses. Past the high place from where we'd seen the sea a few hours ago, and a container ship riding on it. Atmospheric conditions had changed though. There was no sign of the sea. Nor was there any clue to suggest that you could possibly have seen it from this spot.

We descended the long hill down to the stream and climbed the long slope back up the other side, emerging at last onto the main road on which we lived. As we walked the final few yards to home I grew slightly tense. I braced myself for the possibility that we might see Michael's Range Rover on the driveway: that due to some unforeseeable circumstance he might have returned early from work. But Michael's car wasn't there. I felt myself sigh silently with relief. I sensed that Tim was feeling a similar relief. There was no reason why Michael's son shouldn't have gone out for a walk with me on a sunny afternoon, of course. But it had never happened before and it would certainly have given Michael something to think about. I clasped Tim's hand for a second and for a second he clasped mine back.

We went into my house. I put the kettle on. By the time I emerged from the kitchen Tim was standing in the living-room with his clothes off. 'We'd better go upstairs,' I said. 'We can   have our tea in bed.'

106

So we did. We snuggled under the duvet and fondled and caressed each other, rubbing each other's calves and thighs and buttocks, exploring necks and shoulders and cheeks. We touched each other's dicks and bollocks too but didn't try to make each other come again. After all, we'd already done that twice. But we were careful not to fall asleep. Tim needed to be home before his father got back; he needed to be showered and teeth-brushed, and assembling ingredients for his pasta dish.

We had the shower together. And as we lathered each other up, and painstakingly washed behind the foreskins of each other's cocks the urge to do a bit more than that grew on us again and our cocks got stiff...

We brought each other off remarkably quickly, given that we'd last come just two hours earlier. Then we got dressed and Tim prepared to depart. 'Remember to clean your teeth as soon as you get home,' I admonished.

'I will, Will, I promise,' he said, and gave me a kiss. Then, 'When can we next...?'

'I'm going up to London tomorrow,' I said. 'I've promised to meet a friend for lunch. And I suppose Sunday's out, with your dad at home and all that...'

'Can you wangle another day off work next week?' Tim asked. 'Then tell me which day it is and we can sort something out.'

'I'll do my best,' I said. Then I walked to the front door with him and saw him out, giving his departing bottom a playful little spank as he went.

'Email,' he said, turning back just before disappearing round the corner of the house. 'And I love you.'

'Oh darling, I love you too,' I said. I had to stop myself running after him to his own front door and giving him yet another hug and kiss on the step.

My house seemed very empty when I got back inside it. I thought about what I would have for my own supper and rummaged in the deep freeze for a minute. There was no need, though, to decide just yet. It was still warm out of doors and the cuckoo was still calling from somewhere in the vague distance. I poured myself a gin and tonic and went out and sat in the sunshine, alone at the garden table that had once been mine and Aidan's but of which I now had outright ownership.

After a while I could hear, through an open window, the sound of Tim being busy in his father's kitchen. A little after that I heard Michael's car draw up. And then a few minutes later I heard the house phone ring and had to get up out of my seat and go and answer it. It gave me Michael's voice.

I felt a stab of anxiety – or fright – or guilt. But Michael said, 'Tim asked me to ring you.' There was a trace of puzzlement in his voice. 'He wanted me to ask you to join us for supper in a bit. Umm … he's cooking it. A tuna and pasta dish apparently. I don't know if…'

'I'd love that,' I said. More than anything in the world at that moment, actually. Though I didn't say that.

ELEVEN

'It was a wonderful evening,' I said. 'Just the three of us. Like a family. We ate at the dining table, which I know they don't often do, but there was nothing stuffy about it. The pasta dish managed to be both light and filling. Fresh basil and Parmesan scattered over the top...'

'Light and also filling?' Gary said disbelievingly. 'You're obviously a very long way down the road. But if your little boy wonder has cheffy leanings you'll need to break it to him gently that the Italians do not scatter cheese on pasta dishes that have fish in them.' He took a forkful of soufflé from the ramekin dish in front of him and waved it warningly in my direction before popping it neatly into his mouth.

'I'm just saying that he made the dish very palatable,' I said. 'It was a major contribution to the success of the evening. And I put Parmesan on pasta dishes containing fish when I do them myself.'

'Ah,' said Gary. 'You're obviously way beyond redemption yourself. You'll have that in common for the future. A little kink to enjoy sharing when you eventually tie the knot.' He took another forkful of soufflé and I took a forkful of mine. We were lunching at one of Gary's favourite places near the opera house in Covent Garden.

Then Gary's expression changed. 'Being serious for a moment, though. You're treading on very dangerous ground. Having a crush on your best friend's son is one thing – and his having a crush on you – I accept, obviously, that he has a crush on you too – but you can't really entertain the thought of anything lasting coming from it. The situation just won't allow that. His age – or lack of it. Your relationship with Michael – which you've spent two years telling me is the most important thing on your planet. You're taking the most dangerous risk with that.'

'I know,' I said unhappily. I did know. But hearing it spelled out in such bleak terms by another trusted friend was ramming the point home in a way that was unsettling and upsetting.

Gary hadn't finished. 'And even if you're prepared to take a calculated risk with your most precious relationship – if you can accept losing your beloved Michael as a consequence of getting involved with his son – there's the question of the relationship between the two of them. You could end up driving a wedge between a son and his father, leaving them estranged from each other and both adrift in life…'

'Oh God, stop!' I was suddenly on the edge of tears. Gary saw that and he did stop.

'Sorry,' Gary said gently. 'I didn't mean to upset you. I just felt I ought to point out something I was afraid you might not have thought about.'

'As any good friend should. And I thank you for that. Yes, I have thought about those things. They do worry mc. Kccp mc awakc at night. But what can I do? I can't simply turn the switch off and unplug the thing. Relationships don't work like electric lights.'

Gary sighed. 'I know that, of course. That's why they get you in more of a mess than any electric lght. We've all been there; we've all done it. It's just that when you see it happening to someone else...'

'All I can do is enjoy it while it lasts, I suppose,' I said. 'It'll run its course, because Tim will grow out of me. It'll all be over by October anyway, when he goes to university. New people – boys or girls or both – a new life.'

'October's a very long way away,' Gary cautioned. 'Can you really see yourselves, Tim and you, managing to keep Michael in the dark about it for another six months? He's already seen things change between the two of you in just a few weeks. You driving Tim to college and back. Tim taking it into his head to invite you round for dinner...'

'We behaved impeccably last night,' I said. 'No flirting at table, no prolonged eye contact, no sniggering at private jokes...'

Gary rolled his eyes. 'I should bloody hope not...' The waiter came and removed our empty ramekins. 'Thank you,' Gary said.

'After dinner we sat around the living room talking for a bit. Michael and I had a second glass of wine, Tim didn't. (He just had the one, at the table.) He stayed with us and chatted. Till I left quite promptly at nine o'clock. I thought discretion was the order of the day. Better not to try and make a night of it, I thought.'

Chicken escalopes were arriving. This time I said thanks to the waiter.

'Discretion?' resumed Gary when the waiter had gone. 'Tim inviting you round for a meal was hardly discreet. He's only eighteen, though. You can hardly expect him to be...' He interrupted himself. 'Does Tim often sit with you and Michael in the evenings and chat?'

'Hardly ever,' I said.

'Well, Michael will certainly have clocked that. I'm just saying: for God's sake be careful. And you'll have to do all Tim's being careful for him as well as your own, because Tim's too young to know the meaning of it. Because when October comes and takes Tim away – on the wind – to university at the other end of the country, you and Michael are going to need each other more than you've ever done up to now. But if by that time you've blown that relationship...'

'Oh please don't go on,' I said. 'I do know that. Maybe we could talk about something else for a bit.'

'Yes, of course,' Gary said. 'I've no business lecturing you. You can tell me what's happened to this Simon chap who you had on my sofa but who I've never managed to meet.'

I was grateful to Gary for changing the subject. I was more than happy to give him the details of our two more recent encounters. But of course the story came back to Tim in the end. I had to explain that I'd agreed to give Simon up at Tim's request.

'I see,' said Gary thoughtfully. 'That's very noble of you. But does Simon know that?'

'Not yet,' I said. 'I haven't contacted him since that happened. But he hasn't contacted me either. So my resolve hasn't yet been put to the test.'

'Well, whatever happens, you can be assured my sofa is still at your disposal. If you need to entertain either Simon or Tim on it. Or even Michael, though I can't easily imagine that situation arising...'

'The offer's much appreciated anyway,' I said. 'A greater love hath no man than this: that he lay flat his put-u-up for his friend.'

'Michael might be a bit long for my sofa, though,' Gary said reflectively. 'But next time you want to make use of it with any of the above I'll hope to have the chance to say hallo at some point.'

'I promise,' I said. 'Is your chicken all right?'

'Excellent,' Gary said.

*

We went to a film after we'd finished our leisurely lunch, then had a light tea before we split. By the time I got home it was dark. The light in Tim's room was on and so were the downstairs lights. I didn't go up to the door and knock.

I watched some TV and drank a can of beer. Not until it was nearly bedtime did I remember that I hadn't checked my emails since early that morning. There had been nothing from Tim at that time. But now there was.

Hi Will

Yesterday was wonderful. Pity you had to leave so early in the eve. Which day can we spend together next week? I missed you today.

With All My Love

Your Timmy xxxxxx

I was a bit bowled over by that. Especially the valediction.

Gary was right. I was in deep, deep, deep water. And by October hearts would be broken. Certainly by October, maybe much sooner. Not one, not two, but three of them. My heart. Michael's heart. Timmy's...

I clicked on reply. I began,

My Darling, Darling, Darling Timmy...

TWELVE

All we could do for the next three days was exchange emails and know that the other was for most of the time just ten or twenty metres away. Actually, if I opened my bedroom window at night and Timmy's window was also open I could smell the faint sweet trace of him on the breeze.

At least I was able to let him know, by text at midday on Monday, that I had arranged to get the day off on Wednesday. That was less than forty-eight hours away by then: it was a time-scale that seemed manageable. Not that that stopped us wanking, and telling each other about it in detail in our emails.

Wednesday came round at last. Michael drove off to work early and Timmy appeared on my doorstep soon after eight thirty. He was immaculately and appealingly dressed just as he'd been when he'd come round five days before. But even more quickly I took his clean clothes off him, actually undressing him in the hallway so that he ended up standing naked and erect on the doormat. Then I did what anyone would have done and took him straight up to bed. We didn't waste time discussing the sensitive issues around fucking. We cuddled and wanked each other under the duvet. Then when we had both climaxed we went to sleep together, enfolding each other with the arms of Morpheus.

We awoke at around eleven o'clock. Made coffee and

drank it walking round the garden. There was a noticeable change in the weather. In the last couple of hours the wind had changed suddenly and was blowing from the south. Encouraged by a bright spring sun the temperature had risen several degrees. It would have been warm enough to take our shirts off had we been wearing them.

'What would you like to do with the rest of the day?' I asked.

'What about a drive to the sea?' Timmy said. Given that we lived so close to the coast it was a modest enough request. We discussed the various beaches within easy reach. We agreed on one that would not be full of people at this time of year, and that had a welcoming pub not far from it. It was just eight miles away but that was far enough for us to be reasonably safe from the curiosity of people who knew us. At least we hoped so.

'I just need to get something from the bedroom,' I said and nipped upstairs. I took a couple of condoms from the bedside locker, some lube, and a handful of tissues, just in case.

I drove. We went shirtless, though we had jeans on, not shorts. The sea appeared after a couple of miles, winking at us through trees from the distance. Then it disappeared again as we threaded our way downhill towards it. But we didn't lose faith in its beckoning earlier glances and at last it appeared again when we arrived almost on top of it.

'You always make sure we go somewhere there's a pub,' said Timmy as the beachside local came into sight a moment later.

'Of course,' I said. Though this would be only the third time we'd gone to a pub together.

The pub was busy but the beach beyond its windows wasn't. Though it was early we ordered a sandwich each to go with our pints of bitter and sat out in a glass-screened garden. The glass screen gave us the best of both worlds. It brought the sounds and scents of the sea air to us along with the sunshine but left the wind's velocity on the other side of it.

'I liked the way you wrote your story,' I told Timmy between mouthfuls solid and liquid. Though I had already said this in my replying email. 'I had to smile, though, when I read about your fear, concerning your first fuck, that you'd make a pig's ear of it. I could just see you sitting there thinking hard and searching for a synonym for cock-up.'

Timmy guffawed. Then, 'You're absolutely right,' he said, and grinned sheepishly. 'Cock-up was the first word that came into my head. But I knew you'd laugh if I wrote cock-up – in the circumstances. It took me ages to come up with another expression.'

'Well done for succeeding,' I said. 'And though you wrote the piece beautifully, can I give you one tip about layout?'

'What?' he asked doubtfully.

'It's only something your English teacher would have told you years ago but you've forgotten. Try to begin a new paragraph each time a different person starts to speak.'

'Ah,' he said. 'Yes, I did forget that sometimes. I got carried away by what I was writing.'

'Not unnaturally,' I said. 'No harm done, though. But it makes it easier to follow dialogue if you remember. Easier to see who's speaking.'

'Of course,' he said.

'It also carries the bonus of making your text look longer than it actually is,' I added. 'If that's one of the things you're after.'

'I'll remember that,' he said.

'Good,' I concluded the lecture.

A moment later I saw Timmy go rigid like a dog that's spotted a rabbit. 'What is it?' I asked him.

'I just saw someone… It's OK. Don't worry. Two people… They've gone now.'

I didn't pursue this. If Timmy had spotted people he knew… Had he thought I would also know them he'd have named them. They were gone, anyway.

We came to the end of our beer and sandwiches. 'Walk along the beach?' I said, though it hardly needed saying.

'Yes. Better have a piss first, though,' Timmy said sensibly. 'Not many hedges to hide behind down on the shingle.'

'I'll come with you,' I said. 'Nobody's going to look askance at that. There's no-one here that knows us. I'd forgotten momentarily that Timmy's hackles had gone up at the sight of 'two people'. But they'd long gone, anyway.

A quick look round for the signage... Then we headed towards the gents' together. I went in first and moved towards the urinals. There was a row of four of them. The furthest two were occupied. I made for one of the free ones – the one nearest the occupied ones actually – leaving a space for Timmy in the end one. As he was right behind me he had a view only of my back and the two empty urinals. For a second or two he was unaware of the two people pissing in the other ones.

It all took only a second. I registered the fact that the two back views I was approaching belonged to two lads about the same age as Timmy. I then realised that they had both made a startled movement away from each other. They might – but only might – have been handling each other's cocks as they stood there. Anyway, by now I was standing next to them; it was too late to move away without my reason being obvious; and Timmy slotted in beside me. The two lads glanced in my direction as a kind of reflex, and in doing so spotted Timmy.

'Hey mate!' one of them greeted him. 'How did you

get here?' Then, slightly puzzled, 'You on your own, Tim?'

Poor Timmy. He tried to look cool but was clearly very flustered. 'N…no,' he said. 'I'm with a friend. My dad's neighbour. William, this is Tyler and Danny.'

'Pleased to meet you,' I said, turning the top half of me sideways. I wasn't sure what etiquette was required in this situation but I guessed it was probably not a handshake.

The next bit was difficult. It took ages. For both Timmy and me. As for Tyler and Danny, they had either emptied their bladders already or hadn't come in here to do that in the first place.

'How did you get here?' Timmy asked the other two eventually. Conversation does pass the time, and makes every social situation easier.

'On bikes,' said one of the boys. I wondered whether it was Danny or Tyler.

'Heading back now,' said the other one. Tyler or Danny.

They moved off first, the two lads; and Timmy and I spent a minute or so exhaustively shaking the drops from our foreskins in an unspoken shared wish not to have to catch them up.

Eventually we staggered back out into the daylight. 'Walk on the beach,' I said firmly.

It was breezy but surprisingly warm. Every hour or two of warmth is a gratefully received surprise in the weeks after the end of winter. 'Which was which?' I asked Timmy as we began to walk.

'Danny with brown hair, Tyler with black.'

'Got them,' I said. I thought that was probably as far as that conversation needed to go for the moment.

The shore at that point was steep and shingly. In an easterly, it could be so windswept that it brought tears to the eyes and stung the cheeks. Today, with the wind in the south it was almost balmy. The sea was an indulgent, safe, waveleted blue. A few yachts were out, the sun rendering their sails translucent like in a Monet painting. Far off the power station on the point shimmered like an Arabian Nights' palace.

'That's pissed me off,' said Timmy.

'What has?' I said. Though I knew already.

'Tyler and Danny. Meeting them. They'll say something.'

'Well,' I said. 'They might. But who to? And what? They've both had sex with you. They're going to think carefully before they blurt out things about who else you might be having sex with.'

'Hmm,' said Timmy.

'Think about it,' I said. 'Anyway,' I went on. 'Life is a big succession of threats and worries. It gets worse, not better, as you get older. You worry about love, about money. As you get older you worry about your children, then after they've grown up and left the nest you worry about your ageing parents. Then your own ageing. You worry about illness and the nature of your own forthcoming death.' I took Timmy's hand. 'Sorry,' I said. 'That was all a bit morbid.'

'It wasn't,' Tim said, and I felt his hand squeeze mine a bit tighter. 'You're grown up and I'm not yet. It's right that you should share that.'

I squeezed his hand back. 'The thing is, the thing you need to know is that, even knowing that you've got to die and that all hell will break loose around you in all sorts of ways long before that comes to pass, you need to wrap yourself in a protective bubble whenever you can and make the most of it. The bubble has a name, by the way,' I finished.

'The name being…?' said Timmy, still clasping my hand and pumping it.

I laughed. 'You already know the name of it,' I said. 'You little fox. But I'll say it anyway. It's called *this moment.*'

The tide was low. We descended the shingle slope. It wasn't a straight slope but a shelved one. Winter storms had laid the beach in a series of shelves or, if you like, a staircase with slanting risers and more or less level treads. I thought about saying something. But I realised I didn't need to. We both knew, if foggily, what was

122

going to happen here on the beach.

I thought about making it happen with Timmy looking at the sun-sparked blue sea behind my shoulders. But the lay of the land made that … not impossible, but problematic. I laid him face-down on the edge of one of the storm-surge ridges as if on the edge of a bed. I half-lay, half-stood below him on the slope of shingle and pulled his jeans down just far enough to let his bum spring up.

'You've got to take your jeans down too,' Tim said. He couldn't see me. We were communicating via the back of his head. 'No just getting your dick out and nothing else.'

'Fair enough,' I said, and pulled my jeans halfway down my thighs. 'Will this do?' I asked.

'Can't see,' he said, but I'll take your word for it.'

'None of this will hurt.' I said. 'I promise. But if by any chance I'm wrong about that you just have to say so and everything stops at once. And now, although you can't see this and have to take my word for this too, I'm rolling on a condom.' I did.

His bare bum was peachy and smooth. Those muscles are some of the biggest on the body, yet whenever we feel another person's in this situation they always seem smooth and soft. Perhaps it would be different if they were in the middle of running a marathon or doing press-ups.

I parted Timmy's cheeks and took my first look at the little pink whorl they concealed between them. 'I'm going to put a finger in you,' I said. 'Well moistened. Just relax. Remember that what comes down the chute quite regularly is much bigger than my finger.'

I had found the right words evidently: the Open Sesame formula. I could see Timmy's muscles relax. I spat on my finger and slipped it in gently and played with it inside him for a good minute. Then, 'I'm taking it out,' I said. 'Just keep relaxed. It won't hurt but you might get a second's discomfort.'

'Mmmm.' Timmy registered the second's discomfort.

'Sorry,' I said.

'It's fine,' said Timmy, face down in the shingle. Then, 'Is your finger dirty?'

'Not in the least,' I said. 'And I don't expect my cock will be either. One in ten times that may happen. But we have the sea here. And people have showers in their houses…'

Doctors have techniques for distracting nervous patients when they're about to inject them. We radiologists have been trained similarly: some people are terribly nervous about having their X-rays taken. Result? By the time I'd made that last speech my cock was already an inch or two into Timmy. 'Are you OK?' I asked. I added, 'My darling.'

'Yes,' he answered as if surprised by the fact.

Encouraged, I pushed in further. 'Actually it feels nice,' he said.

I looked up at the crest of the beach as I started to fuck him. No-one was walking along, and we were too far down towards the edge of the waves to be visible from the windows of the pub. If someone did come into view, well, they would see two young men horsing around on the beach. True, we were both naked above the waist and my bare buttocks were also on show. But they would have to look quite carefully from the distance of the top of the beach to register that we were actually having a fuck.

As I went on enjoying my cock and Timmy I realised that I was grinding his cock against the pebbles beneath him. 'Is your cock OK against the stones?' I asked.

'Yes,' he said. It was a bit of a gasp. 'The pebbles are very smooth and warm. It's nice. My prick has dug itself a sort of nest.'

It was such a novel experience – for me as well as Timmy – riding a nearly naked boy on a beach, with seagulls calling overhead and the sigh of the wavelets a little way behind my feet... I was soon ready to... 'I'm going to come,' I said suddenly.

'Me too,' said Timmy in a voice of wonder and astonishment. I registered the fact that he wasn't touching himself. That spurred me on to climax. I pushed myself hard into him, pushing him hard down into his shingle nest and then we both shot our loads at once, Timmy's bum bucking and bouncing like a motorbike going over rough ground fast. At last he stopped moving. He'd finished pumping out.

We rested for a minute, me still inside Timmy, gobsmacked and in awe about what had just happened. Then I pulled out of him, rolled onto my back beside him and pulled the condom off, wrapping it in the tissues I'd had in my pocket, while he watched. I could still barely believe that Timmy had come the way he had, just through being fucked. I wanted evidence. 'Roll back,' I said. 'I want to see your cock.'

He did as I asked. His erection was waning, his dick beginning to flop. But there was a telltale thread of spunk drooling from the tip of it. And in the nest he'd ground out among the pebbles there were glistening stones and smears of pearly white. 'Wow,' I said. 'You're the first person I've ever had sex with who's actually done that.'

'First time for me too,' said Timmy, with a degree of sang-froid that surprised me and made me laugh.

'I was going to ask you to return the compliment here and now,' I said. 'But I guess we'll have to wait a bit for that.'

THIRTEEN

I put the used, wrapped condom in the bin in the pub car-park. Then we were naughty boys. We went back into the pub and had a second pint. Tyler and Danny had evidently left, but the memory of our encounter with them still hung about the place and re-entered our thoughts. 'Are you still worried about what they may say?' I asked.

'To me?' said Timmy. 'Or to everybody else?'

'Both. You might be worried about both.'

'Sticks and stones,' said Timmy. 'As far as I'm concerned.'

'Good,' I interrupted. 'And if you're worried about what they might tell other people, don't be. Because they won't. People in their position don't. They've both had sex with you. People in glass houses…'

'Hmm,' said Timmy, considering this. 'I hadn't thought of that.' He took a hefty swallow of beer. Then he said, 'I don't want this afternoon to end before I've had a chance to fuck you, though. To return your compliment. Is it OK if we go back down on the beach?'

'Blimey,' I said. 'You recover quickly, don't you?'

'It's my age,' Timmy said. The smile of a naughty cherub played about his lips. 'Brimming with spunk.'

'You said it,' I said. It took me back. With a twinge of envy, I must admit.

A few minutes later we were strolling back down the beach. To pretty close to the spot we'd used half an hour earlier. 'Can we do it the other way round this time?' Timmy asked. Well, there were numerous other ways round but I was pretty sure I knew what he was thinking of. He wanted us to be face to be face and I was charmed by that.

I fished in my pocket. 'I brought two,' I said. 'And there's some tissue in here to wrap it in when you're finished.'

He took the condom from me and looked at it. 'Will you put it on for me?'

'You are a baby,' I said, and laughed. I added, 'Yes, of course.'

A minute later we were down on the shingle together, rolling and cuddling on the smooth round stones. For the second time in an hour we pulled each other's denims down, each admiring the upward flick of the other's erect dick. I lay on my back on one of the flat shingle shelves, my head towards the waves. When Tim was in position on top of me he would have a view of the sea behind my head. What a position, I thought enviously, in which to deliver your first fuck!

'Give me the condom,' I said. 'And your cock.' He rubbed himself against me, placing his hard-on against my chest so that I could easily reach it, and I rolled the protcctivc sheath over his delicate, weeping glans and down his shaft.

'Put my legs up over your shoulders,' I instructed. 'Then find your way around inside me with a finger, like I did with you. It'll help to relax me. There's lube in my left jeans pocket – no, my left, not your left – or else just use spit.'

He just used spit.

A minute later his cock was inside me. It slipped in easily. Partly because it wasn't fully grown yet. Partly because, I had to admit – and I did say this to him – my anus was quite well practised at this. 'Wow, that's fantastic!' he said as he gave his first two tentative rod-thrusts.

I said, 'You can go faster and harder if you want.'

'Yeah, when I'm ready to,' he said. 'I'm still just taking in the sight. Your dark brown eyes like cherries, the endless sea sparkling behind your curly head...'

I didn't have that view, but could see it in my mind's eye, and seemed to share his sight. From where I lay, looking beyond his head and shoulders and my up-raised legs and feet, I could see the crest of the beach and just the very top of the roof of the pub. There was nobody about, happily. No-one on the beach ... or on the pub roof.

Like a powerful steam engine leaving a station Timmy began to pick up power and speed. His piston came into sight from time to time as it rammed back and forth behind my balls and rigid cock. Pre-come was drooling heavily from my cock-head and I started to touch myself. 'Hey,' said Timmy. 'Let me do that.'

I let him, thought he didn't find it easy. But somehow he managed it, letting most of his weight be taken by one hand among the shingle while laying the elbow of the arm that was working on my cock on my chest for balance.

Because it was only an hour since we'd last shot our wads it took us both longer than it had that previous time to climax. We'd been going about five minutes when I suddenly saw two people come into sight on the crest of the beach, each wheeling a bike. This time there would be no mistaking the activity we were engaged in. But what could the people do? Stand and stare? Shout ribald comments? Run down to join us? Call the police? I thought all those things unlikely. They would almost certainly pretend they hadn't seen us and go on with their walk.

But I was wrong. When they got a little nearer I was able to identify them as the two friends of Timmy's to whom I'd been introduced while having a piss. They stopped and, with grins on their faces, stood and watched.

I didn't tell Timmy of course. Didn't want to put him off his stroke. After half a minute the two boys, seeing me looking at them, started making wanking gestures in front of their crotches. Then, after glancing left and right, and still somehow managing to stop their bicycles falling to the ground, they actually unzipped and got their cocks out. Within seconds they were both stiff. Then they did abandon their bikes, carefully laying them down flat on the shingle. They stood back up, their cocks still out and stiff, and began to move down the beach towards us, actually masturbating themselves as they walked.

I couldn't guess how closely they would approach us, nor what would happen if they actually came right up. But I suddenly knew what was going to happen next. Following the increase in the tension and excitement of the moment that the arrival of the two kids had caused. 'Timmy, I'm coming,' I said. The words had barely left my lips before I shot over my chest.

'You're making me come too,' said Timmy, his excitement evident in his urgent voice. I felt the swelling of his cock inside me, then the bam-bam of his balls against my buttock cheeks told me his penis was spewing his seed out.

A moment later he collapsed onto my chest, though for the moment he left his dick where it was. Heedless as to how close Tyler and Danny now were I wrapped my arms lovingly round Timmy's back.

The sound of two people clapping nearby startled us. Timmy leaped up from me, his cock pulling out of me like a wine-bottle cork. I sat up quickly. Timmy was sitting up beside me, the condom half on, half off, his deflating dick.

'Well done, mate,' said Tyler, grinning towards Timmy. Then Tyler and Danny laughed. There was nothing unkind about their laughter. A moment later Timmy joined in with it and then I did.

The two boys still had their cocks out, though they were no longer stiff. They dangled rather than stood, though their owners still gave them an occasional little reassuring tweak. I noticed that Danny's dick was circumcised, while Tyler's was uncut. I also realised that the three youngsters were all very familiar with one another's equipment. My deflating penis, though the largest of the four, was the stranger on the scene. Quite apart from my age, I was the odd one out.

I handed a wodge of tissues to Timmy. 'Wrap the rubber in this as you take it off.' I had to rummage in my pocket to get to the tissues but felt no immediate urge to pull my jeans back up. The others were insouciantly showing off their smallish cocks. Where my larger one was concerned I had nothing to be ashamed of. I did check out Timmy's half-shucked condom, though. To my relief it wasn't shop-soiled in the least. If it had been I would not have been embarrassed in front of Timmy (we'd discussed the issue already in an adult fashion) but in front of the other two, whom I'd barely met, I would. Even so, I was glad when he pulled it off and wrapped it up.

Sharing the sight of one another's cocks is a great ice-breaker. Within seconds we were all at ease in one another's company, and Danny and Tyler sat down on the shingle with us. We talked of everyday things, getting to know one another; we didn't talk about sex. After a while I noticed Tyler stuffing his now flaccid and very small cock back inside his jeans. Then Danny did the same. After that Timmy pulled his own jeans up over his naked loins and buttocks and a moment later I followed suit. That seemed to all of us a signal to split into our two pairs and go our separate ways. We all stood up, and walked together up the steep shelves of the beach to where the boys had left their bicycles. They picked them up. We parted at that point. I gave Tyler and Danny a peck on the cheek each – which they returned – and Timmy, following my example, did likewise. Needless to say they also returned his kisses. I wondered whether perhaps that was the first time the boys had kissed one another. Maybe I would ask Timmy this at some point. Maybe I would not.

Back in the car, as we did our seatbelts up, I said to Timmy, 'Well, that was rather nice. A social encounter that could have been awkward turned out quite happily. I think, as far as Danny and Tyler are concerned, our secret's safe.'

'Not that it is a secret,' Timmy said with a swagger in his voice. 'It's our relationship. It's us. I don't care who knows about it.'

I needed to put the brakes on. In a bizarre juxtaposition of events, where the car was concerned I was just taking them off. 'Your dad?' I cautioned. 'People who know him? I still don't think we can go into the Green Dragon together bare-chested and kissing at the bar…' I warmed to this theme as we drove out of the car-park. 'Even your dad and I are careful about being seen in there together. Because of what people might think.'

Although my eyes were fixed on the road ahead I was aware that Timmy had turned to look at me. 'What might they think? I mean about you and dad.'

'They might think we were a gay couple,' I said. 'In fact I've heard that some people have actually voiced that thought. They got shot down in flames, of course. Nevertheless we all live in a tiny village where tongues love to wag. I entirely understand your father not wanting to be thought of as being in a gay relationship when he isn't. It could damage his chances, and reduce his desirability, in the eyes of the female sex.'

'Sometimes I think my father is gay,' Timmy said. He said it very quietly. So quietly that I thought I must have misheard him.

'Pardon?' I said.

'I think sometimes that dad is gay,' Timmy still spoke quietly but he enunciated the words very clearly so that this time there was no mistaking what he'd said. 'Like me. Or at least he's partly gay. Bisexual or whatever people call it. He can't be entirely gay, obviously, or he wouldn't have fallen in love with mum, married her, and had me as a result.'

'Well, there are things to be thankful for,' I said. 'But whatever makes you think he has a gay streak?' I'd seen no sign of such a thing in his behaviour towards me.

He'd brushed off every exploratory advance I'd made to him over the last two years. And he was seeing a woman or two. Not that I saw much of them around the place. One or another would turn up occasionally during the daytime when Timmy was at college. They rarely stayed the night as far as I knew. But they certainly existed, I did know that, and they were not men in disguise. I knew that too. I repeated my question. 'Whatever makes you think that?'

'He's very gentle and sensitive for a start,' Timmy said.

'So are lots of straight men,' I said. 'They often hide that side of themselves but that doesn't mean it isn't there. Being gentle and sensitive doesn't make a man gay.' I was well aware of Michael's sensitive side. That had been very apparent when, just weeks after the death of Tim's mother in a car accident, he had found the greatness of heart to console and comfort me in the aftermath of my own sudden loss of Aidan. Yes, he liked to pretend he was a bit of a rough diamond. That went with the job he did: selling farm equipment to big tough gentlemen of the soil. But I knew all about his sensitive side.

'Also,' Timmy went on, ignoring my argument, 'there's his attachment to you.'

'Really?' I said. I mean, I knew he was deeply fond of me, though in a platonic way only. But it was a surprise to hear this being pointed out to me by his son.

'When he talks about you it's very obvious that you're one of the most important people in his life.' When he talked about me? What sort of things did he say when he talked about me? I decided not to ask.

'That's lovely to know,' I said. In a day of wonderful things happening, this was yet another wonderful thing. 'I'm very touched. But…' I had to keep reinforcing my point. 'That still doesn't make him gay. I spend a lot of time alone with him, in quite intimate settings. Sometimes we have a lot to drink. To be honest with you I've sometimes wished he was gay and looked for signs that he might be, but I've seen no sign at all.' I didn't go so far as to say that, among other experiments that came under the heading *looking for signs* I'd once drunkenly grabbed Michael's cock and been rebuffed. I did wonder though, as I spoke, for whose sake I was anxious to make the point that I didn't think Michael was gay: Timmy's? Or my own?

'Well, maybe you're right then,' said Timmy. 'But I can't help noticing that if I have Tyler or Danny over to the house – and when we all went for a meal on my birthday – he looks at them in a way that's sort of admiring. The way a gay man of his age – your age – would look at them. The way that you were looking at them both just now.'

'Me?' I spluttered, laughing.

Timmy laughed too. 'Don't deny it. You were in heaven. Surrounded by three boys with their cocks out. I saw the way you were looking at those two. Well, that's

136

the way dad looks at them.' I listened to all this with astonishment. But astonishment was nothing to what I felt when I heard the next thing he said. 'It's the way dad looks at you.'

FOURTEEN

My mind was in a whirl as we drove back home. I tried to focus only on the day that Timmy and I were enjoying, and on trying to ensure that the remaining hours before Michael's return from work put an end to it were not an anticlimax.

Timmy evidently had the same thought. When we approached our two houses and I was signalling for our turn into the driveway, he said, 'You've never been up to my bedroom, have you? Can I invite you up there now?'

'Yes,' I said. 'That'd be lovely. Though I have seen inside your bedroom before.'

'Really? When…? How…?'

'It was when you were very small. Aidan and I were visiting your parents one evening. Your mother took us upstairs and opened your door. We stood very quietly in the doorway and saw you asleep in your bed. You looked very sweet. I guess you were about nine.'

'Wow,' said Timmy. 'And I never knew.' He chuckled at the oddness of life.

We were getting out of the car now. Timmy led the way to his front door and let us in. He took me straight upstairs. Then there I was in my lover's bedroom. Though much of the space was taken up by a big glossy computer the room as a whole had not yet put away childish things. There were plastic dinosaurs promenading along the window ledge in single file. Toy soldiers, some with rifles or machine guns, were clinging to their positions atop the chest of drawers. I smiled at Timmy. It was the kind of smile that came from an ache inside. 'I love your room,' I said.

'I love you,' said Timmy.

'And I love you too.' I hugged him tightly as we stood beside his single bed. I asked him, because it was important for me, as his lover, to know, 'Are you sore?'

'Sore?'

'Between the legs, I mean,' I explained a bit over-delicately.

Timmy snickered his understanding. 'No,' he said. 'Thank you for asking, but I'm fine. You were very gentle and nothing's sore. What about you? Are you sore?'

I wondered for a split-second if it would flatter him and the size of his cock if I lied and said I was. But I realised that it wouldn't. He would be upset if he thought that he had inadvertently hurt me. I told the truth. 'No, I'm not sore.'

As one we tumbled, locked together in our embrace, onto his single bed.

*

'Who's cooking tonight?' I asked a little later, as we

sipped cups of tea in the garden at the back of Timmy's, Michael's, house. 'Not that I'm after another invitation,' I added quickly. 'Last week was lovely, but we mustn't make things too obvious.'

'Dad's cooking,' Timmy said. 'I cooked last night. But do come and join us if you want.'

'Thanks, but I'd better not. For reasons already given. But I'll invite you and your dad both round for a meal at mine some time soon. That'd look more natural – simply returning last week's invite.'

A blackbird alighted in the tree above our heads and began to sing its rich, loud song. Then my phone rang in my pocket.

'Sorry,' I said as I answered it. It was Simon

'Easter weekend coming up,' he said. 'I'm going to be down at my parents' for a couple of days. Any chance of seeing something of you?'

'Ah,' I said. 'That could be difficult. Remember young Tim from next door?' Simon grunted to show that he did. 'Well, it's turned out that we're having a bit of a thing together. And he rather wants it to be exclusive...' I turned to Timmy and whispered, 'It's Simon. Remember Simon...?' Timmy nodded. His mouth opened but rather vacantly. He looked like someone who wants to say something but doesn't know what it is. 'He's going to be in Westbourne over the weekend.'

I returned my attention to Simon via my phone. 'So it

looks like I can't…'

Timmy interrupted me. 'I wouldn't mind it if the three of us met up…'

'Hang on,' I said to Simon. 'I've got Timmy with me. He's saying, what about the three of us meeting up? I don't know… I have to say I don't think there'd be any sex involved,' I added primly.'

I turned back to Timmy. 'You'd have to explain to your dad that you were going off with two gay men – if we fixed something up. Are you sure…?'

'I think I can handle that,' said Timmy.

Simon seemed to think this tentative plan an attractive prospect, to judge from the sound of his voice. Even if there wasn't going to be any sex. I explained that Timmy would need to fix things with Michael (who might have his own plans for himself and his son over the holiday weekend) before we could make a definite arrangement to meet. Simon said he was fine with that. 'Talk again tomorrow,' he said. 'See what's possible and what isn't.' We ended the call.

*

The next day turned out to be my weekly evening drink with Michael. It was a moveable feast: not always on the same day of each week. This week we were at my house. Timmy was not present.

'Timmy tells me he's going off with you and a gay

friend of yours for a drink tomorrow,' Michael said, extending his long legs across the carpet.

'That's right,' I said. 'My friend Simon who I was with when we gave Timmy a lift in the car that time.'

'Your London pub pick-up, you mean,' said Michael, grinning at me teasingly.

'OK,' I said. 'Yep, that's the one.'

'So how did that come about?' Michael said, a slight frown appearing on his forehead.

Fortunately Timmy and I had agreed our story in an exchange of emails the previous night. 'I happened to be chatting to Tim on the driveway the other day. Simon phoned while we were talking. They remembered each other, and the arrangement sort of made itself.'

'Yeah,' said Michael, crossing his legs. 'That's more or less what Timmy said.' Then why had Michael asked me? Because he was puzzled by the arrangement obviously, if not downright suspicious of it. Timmy and I were skating on ever thinner ice as far as Michael was concerned. It might only be a matter of time before he found out about us. My friend Gary had warned me in no uncertain terms what he thought would be the consequences of that.

I wanted to change the subject if I could, but was afraid that if I did it too abruptly Michael would become even more suspicious. So I half changed it. 'I wonder if you and Tim would like to come and have a meal with me one evening next week. I've got a leg of lamb in the freezer. Too much for one. It needs using up.'

Michael said a provisional yes to that. We'd fix a definite date nearer the time. For the rest of that evening we chatted happily and lightly of other things. I kept looking carefully at Michael to see if he was looking at me with adoring eyes, as Timmy had suggested he sometimes did. But there was no sign at all of that, however hard I looked. I found that I was looking at Michael with adoring eyes instead.

*

It worked out well. Simon and Timmy and I were all free that Good Friday, while Michael had to work. So there was no question of leaving Michael out of things, to mow the grass and twiddle his thumbs on his own while we others went out to enjoy ourselves.

We met in town. I drove Timmy the short distance while Simon took the train along the coast. We'd arranged to meet in a pub in the Old Town behind the beach. Timmy and I got there first but Simon materialised just a few minutes after us. We were all three of us a bit wary of each other, conscious of the new triangular moment that had been born between us. As we sat over our beers at a table outside in the sunshine I found myself focusing on the fact that, although we were of three different ages, we were all almost exactly the same height. If by any chance we did end up in an intimate sexual situation we would make a very cosy fit. It was a great many years since I'd last had a threesome.

I'd rather forgotten how one went about it…

Simon and Timmy were getting to know each other a little shyly. Where do you study? Isn't the weather good? Et cetera. Treading gingerly around the most obvious thing they had in common: that they'd both had sex with me. We got near the end of our midday pints. I didn't think it would be a good idea to go on sitting here downing beer for ever. Not only was I the senior – so supposedly the most responsible – member of the party, I was the only one of us who would have to drive afterwards. Eventually I said, 'Why don't we get some fish and chips and eat them on the beach?'

Nobody had a better idea than that, so we got up and walked back down the street – it was barely a hundred metres – to where the net sheds stood at the top of the beach, with the fishing boats beyond, and where there was a line of fish and chip shops.

Fish and chips here were about as good as fish and chips ever get. All three of us knew that. The catch was landed just twenty metres from where we queued for our portions. You couldn't ask for fresher cod or hake than that.

Taking our open paper-wrapped bundles – salt and vinegar liberally dashed and splashed on top – we ambled down between the net sheds onto the shingle beach. Geographically speaking it was the same shingle beach that Timmy and I had fucked each other on two days ago. That had happened just a few miles up the coast. But here was no remote country area with just a lone pub in sight. We were on the town's main beach, with dozens of people walking about. With professional fishermen preparing their boats for the sea and amateurs sitting on the breakwater and casting lines into the swell. There would be no question of the three of us getting naked and romping together – fucking, sucking and wanking together – on this beach. Instead we walked sedately, eating our fish lunches with our fingers, while a thousand gulls flapped around, surrounding us, in the hope that we'd be nervous enough to spill our meals onto the shingle … as no doubt many people, unnerved by the unexpected situation, did. It was like a scene from that old Hitchcock movie, The Birds.

But we were all locals. We knew how the gulls behaved here and kept our cool, managing not to, accidentally, surrender our lunches to the overwhelming mob of birds.

We were just finishing our meals and looking around for a bin in which to chuck the greasy warm wrapping paper when I spotted a figure, one among many that were criss-crossing the beach, waving to us. It was none other than Tyler. He didn't have his cock out but I recognised him nevertheless.

A few seconds later we all met up. Simon and Tyler got introduced. There was no sign of Danny but none of us commented on that. The four of us drifted along the beach together, chatting, with no particular destination in view. Then Tyler said, 'We're just a few minutes from my place. The parents and my sister are all out. Do you want to come up?'

It turned out we did.

Tyler found a half-full bottle of Kirsch in his parents' drinks cabinet and poured us all a glass of it while the kettle brought itself to the boil for instant coffee. As the nearest thing to a responsible adult among the party I did feel a bit uncomfortable about the raid on the drinks cabinet. Tyler's parents were probably not much older or richer than I was. But Simon didn't seem bothered, so I decided not to be bothered either.

We chatted over our coffee and liqueur. The conversation came round inevitably, neither indecently quickly nor too tediously slowly, to the subject of sex. Tyler asked Simon how he and I had met. He was treated to the story of that meeting – though without every graphic detail – and of how we had ended up together on the sofa of a friend of mine whom Simon had still not met. Tyler thought that quite funny.

'Last time I met these guys,' he said to Simon, 'and it was just two days ago, they were down on the beach just a few miles away, fucking each other for the whole world to see, out in the open in broad daylight.'

'Well, that's giving away our secrets in shovel-loads,' I said good-humouredly. I wasn't sure how Timmy would take this breach of confidence. I needed him to know that I at least was reasonably cool with it.

'Who was giving it to who?' Simon inevitable asked. I mean, anyone would.

'Tim was fucking William,' Tyler answered before

either Timmy or I could speak. 'I think it was his first fuck.'

I could sense that Timmy was getting embarrassed now. To take the spotlight off him I said to Tyler, 'And how would you know that, I wonder?'

'Because... Because...' Tyler stopped, embarrassed himself now, but he had the grace to laugh at his own embarrassment. After all, it was he who had got himself into it. 'Obviously, William, you know the story.'

'I take it,' said Simon, 'that you two...' he nodded towards Tyler and Timmy, '...are pretty intimate.'

'That was a while back,' said Timmy in a suddenly chilly voice. He was clearly getting upset by the way the situation was turning.

'What... Three weeks now is it?' said Tyler to Timmy.

Simon was sitting next to Tyler on the sofa. 'Take it easy,' he said to him quietly. He took the opportunity to put his hand on Tyler's thigh as he said it.

Timmy, who was sitting a little way away from me, in an armchair, now looked directly at me. 'Do you want to take me home, Will?' His face was full of his discomfort.

'If that's what you'd like, then of course,' I said. I wanted so much to call him darling at that moment, but decided not to do so in front of the others. I'd save that for when we were in the car, alone together.

I stood up, not too quickly, smiling. I wanted to keep the atmosphere friendly. 'If Timmy wants to go home,' I said, 'then that's what I want too.' Turning to Tyler I said, 'Lovely to see you again, and thanks for your hospitality.' I looked at Simon. 'Will you be all right here? Do you want running to the station?'

Simon grinned back at me very happily. 'I don't need running to the station. I think I'll be all right here for the moment.'

'Good,' I said. 'See you again soon, I hope. And you too, Tyler.'

Timmy grunted his farewells rather less graciously. We saw ourselves out and walked back to the car, along the sea-front amidst a blizzard of gulls, together.

FIFTEEN

I took the leg of lamb from the freezer the day before I was going to cook it and let it defrost slowly in the fridge. I was looking forward to entertaining Michael and Timmy together. I hadn't seen much of them over the rest of that Easter weekend. They'd done things together, gone out in the Range Rover. I knew they'd met up with Michael's sister and her kids: they went to an Indian restaurant, I think.

I only saw Timmy to wave to across the driveway occasionally. Of course we exchanged emails during those days. Though I was a bit more cautious about texting him. If he was with his father then the ping of the text would have alerted him and he'd have been surprised if his son ignored the alert. People routinely ignored email pings on their phones, though, dealing with them at a later, quieter moment.

Timmy didn't offer an explanation – either in the car going home or in his subsequent emails – of why he'd so suddenly wanted to get away from Tyler's flat that Friday afternoon, and I didn't press him for one. I was perfectly happy that he'd done it. I had allowed the idea to lurk at the back of my mind that day that it might be nice to have a threesome involving Timmy and Simon. Though I wouldn't have proposed it. I'd have let Timmy initiate it if by any chance he'd wanted such a development. I would have been less happy about a foursome that included Tyler. Foursomes have a tendency to split into pairings that are unexpected and perhaps unwelcome, causing complications further down the line. I wondered if, perhaps, the same thoughts had been Timmy's and that that was why he'd dragged me away so suddenly. At any rate I was glad that he did, on balance. Especially because his decision included me: he hadn't flounced out on his own... A little internal voice reminded me dampeningly, though, that I had had a car with me; he hadn't.

That I was emailing Timmy twice daily, and he was replying with the same regularity was a source of comfort to me. But it didn't mean that he wasn't also exchanging emails and texts just as regularly with Tyler and Danny. In fact I rather assumed he was, and I didn't have a problem with that. I didn't expect him to tell me details of any such exchanges. Timmy had his friends, just as I had mine. It did go through my mind, though, that Tyler's sudden appearance on the beach just after Timmy, Simon and I finished our fish and chips might not have been a coincidence. Timmy could easily have alerted to Tyler to our whereabouts. I wasn't going to ask Timmy about this.

We were in the final days of Timmy's Easter holiday. I didn't know how easily we would be able to meet up once college had begun again. But this wasn't something that could be discussed over a cosy dinner for three that included Michael.

It was a very civilised evening. We drank a small can of beer each while I put the finishing touches to the dinner, my two guests confidently helping me in the kitchen. Then we sat and ate at the dining-room table, using the best china that had once belonged to Aidan's parents.

(Two weeks before he died, by which time he knew what was happening to him, Aidan asked me suddenly, 'Why can't we have the best china every day?' And from then on, till he was beyond eating solid food, we did. Though it had brought tears to my eyes every time I got the plates out from the stack. Since his death I'd used those beautifully patterned plates only on the rare occasions I had company at home.)

We talked about holiday plans. Michael hadn't yet decided where he would take Timmy in the summer, he said. The Canaries perhaps. He said, looking for a moment at his son, that he guessed it might be the last summer holiday they'd take together. Timmy would be at uni this time next year. A new world. New friends to take holidays with… In the look that Michael gave his son I glimpsed for an instant his fear of the loneliness that would then be his. Though mixed with it I also saw the infinite love he felt for his son and the deepest tenderness.

As for me… I said I had no plans at present. Since Aidan died my holidays had consisted only of visits to friends. Not that that had been bad. I had one friend who lived in Paris and another in southern Portugal. I'd managed to keep what passed for my tan topped up.

The lamb was judged a success. So too were the roast potatoes and green beans that went with it, and the blackberry crumble that followed. After dinner we sat talking by the fire, a very harmonious family group. We wouldn't be so harmonious, I realised sadly, if – or perhaps when – Michael discovered the truth about my friendship with his son. When at last Michael said, 'Well, that's been lovely but it's time we left you in peace,' I looked at my watch and was astonished to see it was past eleven o'clock.

We all stood up and I saw them to the door together. There was a moment's hiatus while we wondered what form our farewells would take. Then Timmy took the plunge and gave me a big hug. And a quick kiss on the cheek. I didn't dare return the kiss in front of Michael, though he was smiling his surprise at the warmth of Timmy's embrace. But I did hug Michael in front of Timmy, and, reaching up a bit, gave him a tiny peck on the cheek. To my utter astonishment I felt the touch of Michael's lips, brief as a spark, brushing my own cheek. I registered my delight with a tiny rub of my knuckles between his shoulder blades, out of Timmy's sight. Then we quickly un-clasped. Except for final thank-yous and goodnights nothing more was said. But in my imagination I saw myself leaving my cheek unwashed and unshaven for a week.

*

I did shave, of course. I was a medical professional in my own small way, and was expected not to look scruffy or dirty at work. So I washed too, though it grieved me to have to do it. I spent one more day with Timmy during the remains of that Easter holiday. We spent it as we had spent the first one, walking near to home among the fields and woods. The grass and trees had greened up noticeably in the last fortnight, and violets had appeared, bright as amethysts, among the primroses. There were deep crimson orchids. We walked a path alongside a stream. At one point it plunged into a copse. There among the trees red campion grew, hundreds of square yards of it, like a foot-deep mattress of soft green leafage and cerise flower-heads that turned the whole wood red. We threw each other down onto this vast bed and laughingly made love on it. On this occasion we took all our clothes off, even shoes and socks. I laid Timmy on his back and fucked him while we looked smiling into each other's eyes. This time he didn't come spontaneously while I massaged him internally, but he wouldn't let me bring him off. He was saving himself for the return match. Which took place twenty minutes after I'd come inside him. Just time enough for me to relax my relevant muscles. This time I lay down on my tummy and let Timmy take me from behind, in a full reversal of our last week's beach positions. I thought it would be good for him to widen his experience.

Then term started and we couldn't easily meet. We emailed each other nightly, and spoke if we coincided on the driveway. On those occasions we hugged and kissed, and squeezed each other's soft but whelk-tough cocks through trousers if we were certain that Michael was not about. But that was about as far as it went.

Once we arranged that I would pick Timmy up when he had an early finish at college. I drove him to the car-park of the cliff-top pub where I had met Simon a few months back. But I didn't take Timmy into the pub. We made straight for the cliff-side path and walked along it, finding the clearing among the gorse bushes where Simon and I had had sex. There we brought each other off by hand, standing up. We couldn't risk doing much more than that. The gorse – never out of bloom – was at its golden best. And, though we found that kissing was far from out of fashion, the gorse still wore its vicious prickles.

Tim gave me a bit of information on that occasion. 'My friend Tyler had a good afternoon with your friend Simon,' he said. 'Probably just as well we left them to it.'

'Yes,' I said. I didn't elaborate. Nor did I pry for any details that Tyler might have told him. It was enough that I had Timmy. And that I was enough for him: for so I seemed to be. I was deeply lucky.

Surprisingly it was Michael who offered us our next opportunity to be together. He told me during one of our evenings that he was going to be away from home for one night the following week.

'Because…?' I asked nosily.

Michael gave me one of his more twinkly looks. This one was partly mischievous, partly sheepish. 'Opportunity to spend a night at Marlpits.'

I thought I knew the name of his lady friend from Marlpits. 'With Anna?' He nodded. I was on hallo-ing terms with Anna, when our paths crossed on the driveway. 'Does she live alone at Marlpits?' I honestly didn't know the answer to that question. I knew only that Marlpits was a big dairy farm two miles away.

Michael looked very uncomfortable for a second. He said, 'She has a husband.'

'I see,' I said blandly. The husband was obviously going to be spending a rare night away from home, for whatever reason. There was no need for me to tell Michael I'd worked that out. 'Well, good luck,' I added broadmindedly. 'Enjoy yourself.'

'The only reason I'm telling you,' said Michael a bit crisply, 'is that it'll leave Timmy on his own for the night. I know he's eighteen but he's never spent a night in the house on his own before.'

Sure,' I said. I remembered that I hadn't slept alone in a house until was in my twenties. Even then it had been a bit of a rite of passage. 'I won't be away next week,' I said. 'I'll keep an eye on him. I could look in on him just before bedtime… Or, if he wants, he can come over here and sleep in my spare room.'

'Well, that's a thought,' said Michael.

'Just ask him,' I suggested, as if butter wouldn't melt in my mouth, 'which he'd rather. Either way, I'll make sure he's OK.'

Michael wagged a figure in mock warning. 'And either way, no taking advantage of him.' He grinned at me.

I laughed as I was meant to do. 'His virtue will be my first concern,' I said in a jocular tone. 'He'll be safe with me.' The exchange was meant to show that we were so safe in our shared knowledge that my interfering with Timmy would be unthinkable that we could joke about it. On Michael's side the sincerity was total. So was his trust in me. I was the one who was acting it.

I had told Timmy, reassuring him, that not telling his father he was gay did not amount to living a lie. But what I was doing now where Michael was concerned amounted to exactly that. I felt wretched about 'lying by omission' to Michael. But I didn't see how else I could have proceeded.

Hi Will

Dad's told me. Actually I'm not the least bothered about spending a night alone in the house. But I've pretend to dad that I'm a bit scared about it. So I've told him I want to come and stay the night with you. I guess that's what you would prefer too. (At least I hope you would lol)

See you on the night. If not before.

WAML

Your Timmy xxxxxxxxxxxxxx

Arrangements were finalised between the three of us. I asked Michael, pretend casually, if he was eating out

with his married friend Anna from Marlpits Farm. He
said, in a bit of a mumble, that yes he was. Deviously I
asked him where he had in mind to take her. He told me.
I said boldly that in that case I'd take Timmy out for a
Chinese before bringing him under my roof for the night.
Michael looked a bit surprised by that for a second, but
only for a second. 'Yeah. Why not?' he said. It seemed
he was OK with it.

It hurts to be trusted by someone you love, when you
don't deserve their trust.

*

I took Timmy to a Chinese restaurant a few miles
away – in a prudently different direction from the town
where I worked and he went to college. He looked lovely
sitting opposite me at the table. Open-necked shirt, wide
grin, starched white tablecloth… I took a photo of him
with my phone. I couldn't resist it. When he took one of
me too I felt more than flattered.

Back at my house we sat on my sofa. It seemed a
lifetime since we'd first sat here together and hugged,
and exchanged a first tentative grope of each other's
denim-clad crotches. This time we touched each other
only lightly for the moment. We enjoyed a nightcap of
Jack Daniels. (I'd bought a bottle specially, guessing that
Tim would like it. And he did.) And then we went to
bed.

'You've heard of sixty-nine, I guess?' I said when
we'd got undressed and stood facing each other beside

the bed.

'Heard of it,' Timmy said. 'Seen it in the odd porn vid. But never done it.'

I said, 'There's no time like the present.' We half covered ourselves with the duvet – we had to balance keeping warm against being able to breathe – and got on with it.

I had the easier part of it. My mouth took Timmy's penis easily. On mine he gagged a bit. But it was another first for us and it was special. I buried my nose in his anal musk while tasting, almost for the first time, or for the first time properly, the sweet and sour saltiness of his cock. I was lying on my back, and as I sucked him I stroked his buttocks like someone polishing cricket balls or apples. He, lying on top of me, reached down and stroked the hair on my shins and thighs.

I found myself ready to come before he did. I warned him of the impending shot. To my great surprise he went on sucking. He swallowed me down without complaint. As it was the first time he'd given anyone a blow-job… Well, I gave him full marks for that. I felt greatly complimented. And when he came himself a minute later… I swallowed what he pumped into me and savoured it. I could hardly have done anything else.

But the best part was still to come. We went to sleep together. Cuddled, half waking, half sleeping, throughout the short night. I'd set the alarm prudently. But we had no need of it. We both woke a few minutes before it was due to go off. We found ourselves looking into each other's eyes along the pair of pillows. 'I love you,' I said.

'I love you too,' Tim said.

'Got to get you up for school in a minute,' I said, though making no effort to get up myself.

He smiled into my eyes. 'That was the best ever,' he said.

'Yes,' I agreed. 'The best yet.'

SIXTEEN

Darling Will

*I may not be able to see you so often from now on.
Things happen. Life is life.*

With Love as always

Timmy xxx

All of it made sense. I couldn't disagree with any of it.
The email filled me with great foreboding nonetheless.

Days passed. Michael and I had our weekly get-
together. He phoned me a few minutes beforehand. 'It's
supposed to be my turn to invite you. Is it OK if I drop
round to yours instead? I can bring a bottle if you like.'

'No need,' I said. 'I've got plenty. Just bring yourself.
I'll stoke the fire up. See you in ten…?'

'Make it twenty,' he said.

'I'll have the fire roaring,' I said.

Michael arrived exactly twenty minutes later. He
looked a bit tense around the mouth. But he took his
usual seat by the blazing fire and nodded as I poured a
glass of red wine for us both. Then he said, 'Bit of news
our end. Uhm… Timmy's told me he thinks he's gay.'

'Ah,' I said. There was a moment's silence. Then I
said, 'I remember you once telling me you'd be totally

supportive of him if he was.'

'Yes,' Michael said. 'And I will be. Actually … I wasn't totally surprised to hear him tell me. Little things I'd noticed.' I felt an urgent need to ask what those little things were. But the need to bite my tongue was even more urgent. Michael continued. 'But it was brave of him to come out and say it. In an odd way I find I almost love him even more because he has.' That announcement melted my heart. I knew that Michael's love for his only son was already boundless.

'When did he tell you?' I asked.

'Early this morning,' Michael said. 'Before he drove off to college. We had time to talk for a few minutes but not to go on about it for hours. He got the timing about right. He's a clever lad.' A tiny pause. Then, 'I asked him if he'd like to talk to you about it. He said very sweetly that he didn't need to specially. It would come out in the natural course of things, he said.'

'Very sensible of him,' I said. I was managing to keep calm. Managing not to panic.

'He's got a boyfriend,' Michael said.

I felt myself go hot and cold. The blood in my veins turned to ice-water, yet I was afraid I was starting to blush. 'Who?' I asked in the voice of a ghost.

'Remember when it was his birthday there were two lads, two of his college friends, came out with us? It's one of them, apparently.'

Danny and Tyler. 'Which one?' I asked. I was trying to turn my face into a mask.

'Which one?' Michael frowned and looked puzzled. Only then did I realise that you don't ask 'Which one?' about people you've never met or heard things about. But Michael's brow cleared. Evidently he'd quickly worked out that Timmy must have talked to me about who his close friends were, and decided that it was not unreasonable for me to know who was who. 'A chap called Tyler,' he said.

'Oh right,' I answered, feigning a lack of any deep interest, while inside me my whole world fell apart.

*

I didn't get any emails from Timmy. I didn't send him any. I couldn't think what to write. Days passed. Our paths crossed once on the driveway by accident. Timmy tried to smile timidly at me but couldn't manage it. He had to look away again. I'd managed to smile at him, but neither of was able to speak.

I did email him after that.

Dearest Timmy

Michael has told me about your coming out to him. I think you were very brave to do that and admire you for it. I know he's right behind you. So am I. I also know about you and Tyler. I think that's great news and I wish the pair of you all the joy in the world and all the luck.

Come in for a chat any time you want. Bring Tyler if you like.

Love as ever

Will xxx

I could write at this point that it cost me a lot to say that. But it didn't. My coffers were empty. I had nothing more to lose. I had already paid the full price of loving too well but unwisely and bestowing my heart in the wrong place. In the weeks that followed I had the feeling that I had lost Aidan all over again. That I'd now been widowed twice.

I did get a reply to my email.

Dear Will

You are very sweet. Thank you for your understanding. And for everything else. Thank you for being you in fact.

Timmy xx

I had to be content with that.

Michael could see that I wasn't my usual self during the following weeks. He asked me, week after week, if anything was up. I said each time that there wasn't. He knew I wasn't telling the truth but he didn't pursue it relentlessly. He just opened the door gently each week. He didn't try to push me through it. But his goodnight hugs each time were stronger and more supportive. Though he didn't return any of my kisses, he often hung about in my arms long enough for me to kiss him twice. Of all the people in the world Michael was the one I would have wanted most to pour my heart out to. But of all the people in the world he was the last one with whom I could possibly do that.

I told Simon that Timmy and I had broken up. He expressed his commiserations on the phone. But he wasn't coming down to Westbourne in the near future. He didn't suggest we meet up in London on the other hand, so I didn't suggest it either. I made the reasonable assumption that life had moved on for him too, and that he had other, new, things on his plate; new people in his life. As for Gary, I told him the news by email. He too was sympathetic. But there was no chance of our meeting up. His job in television had taken him to the United States for a couple of months.

One dark evening in June (all evenings were dark that late spring and early summer, all mornings likewise, and all afternoons) Michael and I were having our usual chinwag. 'I've got an idea to put to you,' Michael said. 'It might be the last thing in the world you'd want, so just say no if you don't like it…'

'Tell me what it is,' I said.

'We were talking about summer holidays. Well, Timmy wants us to go to Gran Canaria. To a very gay-centred resort. And he wants to bring Tyler along… Of course, if that's what he wants…' Gamely Michael nodded his head though I could see that inwardly he was shaking it. He went on 'But I can't say I'm really looking forward to it myself. I could take a woman along for company, but Timmy tells me the whole place is too gay for that. A woman wouldn't be comfortable there.' He looked at me. A flash of bright blue eyes that reminded me, inevitably, of his son. 'I don't suppose you'd be up for coming along…'

What mixed emotions flooded my thoughts at that moment. A holiday with Michael! But with Timmy and Tyler too?! I hesitated for perhaps a second, then said, 'I'd like nothing better, actually. But only if Timmy and Tyler were happy with the idea. If they had any reservations…'

'It's OK,' Michael said. 'It was Timmy who pestered me to ask you. I didn't want to because I thought you'd say no. He insisted I try you anyway…'

'And I'm saying yes. A very definite yes.'

Michael's relief and pleasure were all over his lovely face. 'And I'm so glad you're saying it.' He topped our glasses up.

*

I sat with Michael. The two youngsters had the pair of seats in front. In our row I let Michael have the window seat. 'Makes a change,' he said. 'Usually I let Timmy have the window seat. You do with a kid.'

'Consider yourself promoted,' I said. 'Today you can be the kid.'

'And on the way back, you?' he said with a laugh.

'Something like that,' I said. 'Anyway, there's not much to see.' Except for cutting across a tiny corner of Brittany and the tip of Galicia, the entire four-hour flight was over water.

'I can watch the clouds,' said Michael. 'Lit by the sun from the top. I like doing that.' I wanted to give his thigh a rub. It was lying right next to mine. But I didn't, of course.

*

We had a bungalow apartment in a holiday complex that included gardens, a swimming pool and a bar and restaurant. I'd been to the southern tip of Gran Canaria before – Playa del Inglés, Maspalomas – and knew what to expect. And Timmy and Tyler had done their homework. But it was a bit of an eye-opener for Michael. I was glad for his sake that I was with him. He'd have stuck out like a sore thumb otherwise. He was glad that I was with him. I knew that, though he didn't say it.

That first afternoon we all just lounged around the pool. I was treated to the sight of the other three in speedos. They were treated to the sight of me in speedos. That was a first on all counts and, as far as I was concerned at any rate, very nice. Timmy and Tyler went into the pool a few times, swam a bit and larked about. Michael and I didn't do that just yet.

'It does notice, rather,' said Michael. 'That everyone's

gay around the place.' It did, of course. Men in ones, twos and threes were parading about among the palm trees, casually putting arms around one another and kissing from time to time, clad in nothing but their swimming briefs. One or two weren't even wearing as much as that. 'Everyone but me,' he added.

'Don't worry,' I said. 'You're with me. Nobody'll notice.'

'I was afraid you might say that,' he said.

In the early evening the four of us headed out. We strolled by the beach, looked lazily at the menus in the windows of the restaurants we passed. We had a beer at a pavement café. Then we came upon it – as I knew we would, and as the kids knew we would. Tyler announced it. 'The Yumbo Centre!' Though the words written a mile high above the entrance were *Yumbo Centrum*, which gave the place a Latin look.

The Yumbo Centre, in case you don't know it, is the size of a huge shopping mall. And in daylight hours that is exactly what it is, even if the goods on sale are fairly gay-oriented and the clientele even more so. After dark restaurants begin to open up then, later, nightclubs of every sort. To meet the varying and sometimes eye-opening requirements, as the night wears on, of every conceivable gay taste.

We had a drink in a bar in the Centre. Then, after a walk around the shops, dived into a restaurant. The diners were mostly British and German gay men. We had steaks. They weren't as rare as Michael and I would have liked. They were napped by any sauce of your choice. The sauces, prepared earlier, stood in huge white plastic buckets on a kitchen shelf that was visible through a serving hatch. I shot an enquiring sideways glance at Michael as we ate. He didn't look as if he was enjoying the experience enormously. I guessed he was making the best of it for Timmy's sake. But he was putting the red wine away a bit more quickly than usual. I interpreted that as a sign of stress. It usually is.

By the time we'd finished dining a few cabaret spots were opening up. We peered, part of a jostling and eager crowd, into the doorway of one of them. On a low dais a middle-aged drag-queen, attired in a white and voluminous wedding dress was giving a lack-lustre rendition, through a microphone which he was holding much too close, of *There I was, waiting at the church*...

'Oh hey,' said Tyler, eager-faced. 'Can we go in?'

Michael looked at me. I knew the look. I saved him. 'Not quite us, is it?' I said. 'But if the kids...'

'Look,' said Michael to the youngsters, 'if you two want to go on in, that's fine. Do that. I think Will and I might take ourselves off somewhere else. Stay out as long as you like. If you fall over coming back and wake us up it doesn't matter. Only one thing matters...'

'What?' Timmy asked.

'Stay safe,' his father said seriously. 'You both know exactly what I mean by that. Have you got the wherewithal?'

'Yes,' said Timmy with a trace of a blush.

'And have you enough cash to get you through the night?'

'Yes,' Tyler said.

Michael turned to me. 'Time to leave them to it, I think.'

We gave Timmy and Tyler a wave as we turned to depart but they didn't see that. They were heading excitedly into the throng, pushing at the starting-gate of their new shared life.

We headed out from the Yumbo Centre into the cooler air of the Atlantic night. The elegant street lamps turned the palm-tree fronds into a magic lattice over our heads, and the stars peered down at us through that. Michael looked at me. 'Where to?' he asked.

'Does it matter?' I said.

For a while we were content just to walk the streets and talk. We'd never done this before. Strolling together at night in a warm climate under lit-up palm trees, hearing the sound of the nearby surf. From time to time we saw the sea down the roads we crossed at street corners. *Saw the sea* exaggerates it a bit. What we saw were the white lines of the surf, rolling towards us inexorably from out of the vast Atlantic dark, then disappearing, only to be replaced by the next and then the next. For a second I took Michael's hand. He didn't respond by clasping it. But neither did he shake it off. I didn't want to milk the moment, didn't want to push my luck. The second's contact over, I let his hand go.

We found a bar that was unlike all the others. It wasn't gay. It wasn't touristy. It was a place where the locals drank. And it was half the price.

I'd spent weeks of unhappiness in the wake of my breakup with Timmy. I'd expected this time to be difficult. Spending a holiday with Timmy whom I'd loved but lost, and with Michael whom I loved but could never have. But as I sat with Michael, drinking wine under the awning of a dimly lit bar beside the sighing surf of the unseen beach, I realised that I hadn't been happier in months. Months? Make that a couple of years perhaps.

Adam Wye

SEVENTEEN

I didn't hear the boys come back. Michael said he didn't either. We both slept like logs. We all got up late and wandered out for breakfast in that first-day-of-holiday relaxed half daze, finding a pleasantly sunlit café where we sat outside on the pavement.

Our bungalow had two rooms. There was a living-room cum bedroom, where the boys slept, and a bedroom off it that was the headquarters of Michael and myself. We had a single bed each, I need to mention at once, and we shared our own bathroom and shower. Michael and I had returned a little the worse for wear the previous night, though long before the boys did, and were ready for sleep at once. It was a pleasant if tantalising novelty to see Michael taking his clothes off. Even if he did it with his back to me. But he slept naked, like I did, and I got a very nice view of his appealing firm buttocks as he hopped in beneath the duvet cover. 'Goodnight,' he said and switched off his bedside light. On the other side of the room I copied him in both. The next thing I knew it was ten o'clock in the morning and the sun was knocking at my eyelids.

I found myself looking thoughtfully at Tyler as we all had breakfast. After twenty-four hours in his company, and taking into account our three previous encounters (during two of which I'd seen and admired his pretty, tasselled cock) I'd come to the conclusion that he was a lovely, beautiful boy, who not only had plenty of charm on the surface but a sound, good character underneath. If I hadn't thought that I would have chafed at the idea of his being with my – my *formerly known as my* – Timmy. As it was I managed to accept with a good grace the fact that I'd lost out to a younger guy. It was evident that Tyler was right for Timmy and Timmy was right for Tyler. At least I had the consolation of the company of Michael for a week. Though that would have its limitations – we weren't going to be having sex together, and that was already causing me some physical frustration – the situation was unprecedented. We were spending our daytimes half naked in each other's company and sharing a bedroom, naked in our separate beds, by night.

The boys had wanted the full English breakfast. Michael and I went along with that. With superior airs we imagined ourselves preferring the local breakfast of coffee and toast with olive oil poured on top of it, but gave in to the kids' wishes of course. And actually the full English, eaten out of doors, under a cloudless blue sky, among palm trees, two thousands miles south from where we normally ate, was more than nice.

Timmy and Tyler wanted to spend the day sunbathing among the dunes of Maspalomas beach. They'd read about it. I'd been there. I'd fantasised about spending time there with Michael, both of us naked, but I knew that it would freak him if I were to take him there just yet. Maybe towards the end of the week… Even then, I had no illusions about the possibility of our having sex together when we got there. Or either of us having sex there with anyone else.

'Actually,' said Michael, looking decidedly uncomfortable (he'd obviously googled the Dunas de Maspalomas too, and knew what they were all about), 'I think I'd rather just chill back by the pool. Bit tired after yesterday.' He didn't look at me but there was an unspoken question in his voice. I knew what the question was. I answered it.

Much as I would have loved to join Timmy and Tyler and frolic naked with them on the beach – with them and anyone else who came along – there was something I wanted more than that. So I wasn't just being dutiful when I said to Michael, 'I'll join you. I'm a bit whacked too. That's what I'd like. That's if…'

Michael did turn to me then. There was a look on his face that humbled me. It spoke of relief, of gratitude. Of something else…? No, I didn't allow myself even to think that.

Then Michael turned back to the kids. 'You got sun-cream? Plenty of it? If you run out and begin to burn, come straight back.'

'Yeah, yeah,' they both answered. 'We got that.'

'And the other kit?'

'Yes dad,' said Timmy, feigning boredom, but I read between the lines of his answer and saw there his happiness that his father cared about the details – and cared about him – so much.

So while Timmy and Tyler headed off towards the sand dunes to have an exciting time Michael and I went tamely back to our bungalow. I was content with that. I would be spending more time close to Michael than I ever had. You take what life has to offer you and, unless you're stupid, you make the most of it.

Yet sometimes, when you think you're in for a boring time, life has other plans. Michael and I got into our speedos in our bedroom... Yes, he insisted on keeping his back to me while he did this, and I failed to catch a glimpse of his cock dangling between his legs, even though I looked out for this with great interest... Then we went out and lay by the pool. We each had a book with us. Michael's was something by Ruth Rendell, which I approved of. I can't remember what mine was.

To begin with we had the place to ourselves. Everyone else in the complex, it seemed, had better things to do and, like Tyler and Timmy, had found more interesting places in which to do them. But then a couple of guys emerged from a bungalow opposite and settled themselves in a pair of sun-loungers just across the pool from us. I guessed they were in their early twenties. The clothes they wore gave nothing away: they weren't wearing any. The swimming pool was a small one. Nevertheless they were still a few yards away from us, separated by the small expanse of water. All the same they were close enough for us to see quite clearly that one was circumcised and one was not.

Each of them had a kindle reader, or something similar, with them and once they had got comfortable side by side on their adjacent loungers they started to read contentedly, leaving Michael and me to stare (if we wanted to) at their nicely shaped legs and flaccid cocks.

In days gone by it used to be easy to read the title of a book that was being read by someone opposite you – in a train, or on a sun-lounger – but these days, when most people read from an electronic device, it was far from easy. You could, if you were curious and had twenty-twenty mid-range vision, amble past their shoulders at a carefully judged distance and catch a glimpse of the text. But neither Michael nor I was interested enough to do that.

What were they reading? Something sexy? Maybe not. But whatever it was, I noticed that after a few minutes each of them had let a hand stray absently towards his dick and was starting to fiddle with it. I didn't alert Michael to this. But I looked sideways at him occasionally while pretending not to, and I did see that from time to time he was glancing across at the action on the other side of the water, then looking quickly back down again at his book.

From time to time the two lads opposite glanced furtively across at us, then each time returned quickly to their reading and their dicks. Then one of them – the circumcised one: I had no other way of distinguishing them – removed his hand from his own dick, which had remained small and flaccid, and commandeered his friend's equally soft organ with it.

His friend, finding his hand displaced from his own

penis then unhurriedly crossed arms with his mate and felt for his cut cock. They went on reading, not glancing at each other, while I went on reading and glancing at them from time to time, hoping not to be caught doing it, and looking at Michael from time to time... Michael was doing exactly the same as I was. Looking at the other two intermittently while pretending he wasn't. Neither Michael nor I had let our hands stray to our own (let alone each other's!) speedo-covered dicks.

I had let my eyes stray to Michael's speedos, though. They now contained a bit of a bulge, ridge-shaped and the size of a small banana. It lay angled towards his hip-bone and quite by chance, though it was a happy chance, it was on the side of him that was nearest to me – where I could see it the more easily.

I looked back at the two young men opposite. They were no longer just feeling each other's dicks but were openly masturbating them. Those dicks were fully erect now, and pointing up towards their owners' belly buttons. Their owners still held their e-book readers in front of them, but were only glancing at them from time to time. They were also exchanging inscrutable looks with each other and – even more regularly – looking over at Michael and me, their brief covert glances at us gradually developing into brazen and extended, though friendly-looking, stares.

By now Michael appeared to have lost his place in his book. He kept glancing down at it, but only when the men opposite were looking at him. When they were not looking at him he was looking at them – with a fascinated gaze. Though I glanced at him often, he was taking great care not to look at me.

I looked down at my own crotch. There I could see a similar banana-shaped ridge to the one that Michael sported – and it lay pointing towards him, as luck would have it, just as his was pointing towards me. Even as I looked at my own cock-ridge I saw a spot of wet suddenly blossom where my speedos encased its tip. A perfectly round spot, the size of a ten-pence piece. I glanced across at Michael's crotch. Since I had last looked there his hardening penis had produced an identical dark spot. I wondered whether our two wet spots were visible to the lads opposite. Whether they'd noticed them. I did a quick calculation. Since I could make out their cock-heads (the un-cut guy's had worked its way out of its foreskin sheath so it was as much in evidence as his cut friend's) the chances were that they could see our wet spots if they looked. And they were certainly looking…

Their mutual wank increased in intensity and speed. Their legs began to jerk about spasmodically and to make scissor movements. I looked again at Michael's crotch – and nearly jumped. He was fully stiff and the end of his cock was visible, pointing towards me, poking pinkly out above the top of his speedos. The pink bit was the shiny wet tip of his glans. His darker, olive coloured, foreskin still sheathed the rest of it. The length of the whole thing now that it was in an extended state was indeed impressive: a good inch and a half longer than mine – even though, when I looked back down at myself

I saw that my own cock's snout was on display too, peering out from my speedos like Michael's was, and drooling a little puddle of wet towards my hip.

The boys opposite became vocal. Both started to grunt. The movements of their hands on each other's cocks became more frantic and their legs thrashed about.

I actually saw their sperm shoot out. First the un-cut one and then the cut. Spurts that landed a little north of their navels – the cut one's actually making it up to his chest. Michael's eyes were fixed on the sight: they were almost out on stalks. His cock-tip was pouring pre-come … like syrup running from the end of a spoon. I did see him glance at my own cock at that point, saw him take in its dimensions, its visible tip and its dribbling state. By now the boys opposite had relaxed, though they hadn't yet mopped up. They half lay, half sat on their loungers, grinning broadly at us. I grinned broadly back.

'Got to have a splash,' said Michael urgently and for a moment I wondered what he meant. It became clear a second later as he leaped up from his lounger, took two paces forward and then jumped into the swimming pool feet first. I was tempted to join him but for the moment hung back. What I really wanted to do, of course, was wank. That that was what Michael also really wanted to do was more than obvious.

Michael splashed water over himself, standing in the pool, then moved into deeper water, got down into it and swam a few strokes. One of the lads opposite called across to me, 'You don't have any tissues on you by any chance?'

I'd brought a small backpack out with us with bits and pieces in it. Tissues included. I fished in the backpack and pulled them out. One of the lads made a move to get up. 'Stay there,' I said, aware of the mess he'd make if he did stand up. 'I'll bring them across.' Which I did. I was with the two lads in seconds, looking down at their slowly deflating cocks. I handed the tissues to the nearer one, the un-cut one. 'I'll let you do the rest,' I said. We all giggled at that.

'Want to come and have a beer with us?' the cut one said. 'You and your mate?'

'Maybe,' I said. 'I'll see what he says. Don't take it the wrong way if he doesn't want to. I have to be a bit sensitive towards him. He finds some of this a bit difficult. He's straight.'

'He's straight?' said the un-cut one. We all looked across the water to where Michael was now re-installed on his sun-lounger, lying back, looking at us with an un-readable expression on his face. 'If you believe that...' The un-cut lad allowed the amused twinkle in his eyes to finish his sentence.

'I know,' I said. 'We'll see. But if we don't join you this time, no hard feelings. Another time perhaps. Right now I'd better be getting back to him.'

Michael didn't want to join the other two for a drink. 'I think I need to get out of the sun for a bit,' he said. 'Do you mind if I go inside for a while? Still a bit tired from yesterday.'

'And from months of hard grind at work,' I said. 'It's called winding down. So of course I don't mind if you want to go indoors for a bit. Uhh… would you mind if I came in too?'

His face, which had looked tense while we spoke, now broke into a smile and he laughed. 'Of course not!'

We walked together to our bungalow. I gave a cheery wave to the other two lads, still lying naked on their loungers, and they waved back. Even Michael managed a shy nod towards them as we left the pool area.

We lay on our beds, still in nothing but our speedos, in the slatted light that came through half-closed blinds. Neither of us was erect now (yes, I looked) but we'd both been very excited very recently and the atmosphere in our room was cloying with testosterone and musky with un-tasted sex.

'Tyler's a nice guy,' Michael said. 'I've been watching him with Timmy. Wondering a bit. But I'm very reassured by what I've seen so far.'

'Same here,' I said. 'You want the best for Timmy, of course. And I've wondered about Tyler a bit too. But you're right. Tyler's lovely. I think he's very right for Timmy. But you know… It's the same with a first boyfriend as it is with a first girlfriend. It's not necessarily going to be the person they end up with for life.'

'I do know that,' said Michael placidly. 'But all the same…'

'Yes,' I said. 'I'd drink to that.'

'Another thing about Tyler,' Michael went on, still in a calm and thoughtful voice, 'is – though I shouldn't admit to noticing this – he's extremely cute.'

EIGHTEEN

Our boys – I mean Timmy and Tyler – returned to the bungalow around six o'clock, to find us lightly sleeping on our beds. They came in and laughingly woke us. They'd had a good time: that was clear from the sparkle in their eyes. Excitedly Tyler started to tell us about their adventures in the dunes. 'We saw two German guys giving each other…'

Timmy cut him off. 'I don't think dad particularly needs to hear this.'

'Hmm,' said Tyler, only slightly deflated. 'But Will might.'

'Yes, I might,' I said, wanting to help him, 'but some time when we're alone together perhaps.' Tyler grinned at me. He'd got the point.

I didn't volunteer the information that we too had been treated to quite a sexy spectacle, and without having to traipse all the way along the beach to see it. I was pretty sure that Michael wouldn't want me to, and that he certainly wasn't going to tell the story himself. He didn't. He said something else, though, which surprised me almost as much as if he had.

'I hope you two were careful.' This in a rather serious tone of voice, although he was still lying on his bed in nothing but his speedos.

'Careful in what way, dad?' Timmy said with a frown.

'I'm talking about sand,' he said, still poker-faced. 'Romping naked among sand dunes. You don't want to find a few grains of that in the wrong place.' Then he cracked a smile and we all laughed.

'We were careful in that respect,' volunteered Tyler. 'If you're not ... well ... whooh ... it doesn't bear thinking about. Easier to be Danny in that situation.'

'Why?' Michael asked.

'He's circumcised,' volunteered Tyler. 'It's one thing less to worry about.'

'I see,' said Michael, and that was that.

This was the first time Danny had been mentioned on the holiday. And before that, because I hadn't been speaking much to Timmy, I hadn't heard his name in weeks. 'How is Danny?' I asked now.

'He's got a girlfriend now,' said Tyler a bit abruptly. Both boys looked a bit tight-lipped for a moment. The subject of Danny was dropped.

*

I found myself on my own with Tyler quite soon afterwards. The four of us were walking together towards the Yumbo Centre in search of an evening meal. Following our rather so-so steak dinner of the previous night Michael wanted to give the two boys a slightly more sophisticated eating experience. He'd read up about a traditional Spanish – specifically Galician – restaurant that was just across the square from the Yumbo Centre. What the boys got up to after dinner was their own affair, Michael said, and we wouldn't be hanging about to cramp their style, but he wanted them to try a proper Spanish restaurant first.

Now Michael was walked side by side with Timmy, chatting, while Tyler and I, a few paces behind them, talked between ourselves. It was the first time we'd had a chance to do this, just the two of us, without the others being party to the conversation. Tyler now took the opportunity to tell me in startlingly graphic language what he and Timmy had observed people doing in the dunes. Plus what they had done themselves. They had taken the precaution of lugging with them a spare bedcover they'd got from a cupboard in our bungalow. That had reduced the sand danger quite a lot. They had each fucked the other on it, and quite a crowd had collected to watch them doing it. I didn't say this but I felt quite pleased with myself for having taught Timmy how to do this. Presumably at some point between then and now he had passed the lesson on to Tyler.

In view of the candour with which he'd described the afternoon's events among the dunes I felt obliged to tell him in some detail what had happened by the poolside, though to spare Michael's reputation in his eyes I didn't describe the sight of his peeping, drooling cock, or his desperate plunge into the swimming pool. But it turned out that I hardly needed to. Tyler said quite casually, 'You and Michael. Have you got it together yet?'

I laughed to cover my confusion. 'Some chance of that,' I said. 'Much as I might like to, there's no way that Michael...'

'Oh come on!' Tyler said.

'Michael's straight.'

'OK, he's straight enough to have got married and produce Timmy – and we're all grateful to him for that – but... Well, that goes for a lot of straight men. You must know that.'

'Yes, Tyler,' I told the eighteen-year-old savant, 'I do know that. But I've known Michael a long time... If I'm honest with you, I've tried it on with him a few times over the years. Without any success.'

'Yes,' said Tyler. 'But for most of that time he didn't know he had a gay son. He had to behave the way he did because he thought Timmy would be straight. Had to set him an example if you like. But now...' Tyler shrugged his shoulders. 'It's a whole new ball-game. The old rules no longer apply.'

'Hmm,' I said. I hadn't thought of that. I was surprised that Tyler had. Had he and Timmy been mulling this over together? 'I'm not sure,' I said, 'whether you have a very wise old head on your young shoulders or if you're just plain wrong.'

'I'm wise,' he said, grinning broadly.

'Time will tell,' I told him a bit more cautiously.

'Call me Ty,' he said.

The restaurant was smartly furnished yet cosy too. Michael was insisting on being properly Spanish. Fino sherries before we started. Razor clams – which none of us had tasted before: they were insubstantial but delicious. Then Segovia-style roast baby lamb and a bottle of Rioja. Manchego cheese, then crème caramel to finish. The boys didn't complain at all but said they enjoyed it. At least they ate it all. Michael and I shared the bill. Timmy and Ty thanked us, then as soon as they politely could they headed across the square to the Yumbo Centre. You could feel that they'd have run across if it wouldn't have looked too ungrateful.

Timmy and Ty had had a good time at the Yumbo Centre the previous night, and clearly they wanted to recapture the spirit of it. For the same reason Michael and I returned, via the beach, to the bar we'd sat outside this time last night. We were greeted in a very friendly fashion by the waiters as always happens if, when you're on holiday, you return to a bar for a second night. They naturally assumed we were a gay couple… Why wouldn't they? Two men of the same age, clearly very fond of each other, holidaying in a gay resort…

Our conversation was different from yesterday's, though. Deeper, somehow. We told each other things that over the past two years we hadn't talked much about. The progression of our careers. Our well-hidden, deeply private self doubts. Michael's thoughts about living on his own for months at a time once Timmy went to university. Our thoughts – mine as well as Michael's

– about the Timmy-Ty relationship.

'You know they've both applied for Brighton?' Michael said.

'No, I didn't.' I said. 'I mean I knew Timmy had, but I hadn't thought about Ty's university choice.' I thought for a moment then added, 'Hoping they can be together, I suppose. While we both know there's a much bigger chance of them ending up in different places. The usual story of university separating teenage sweethearts and tearing them apart.'

'I don't want to see Timmy with a broken heart,' Michael said. He gave me an odd look as he said it. I couldn't interpret it. I knew only that somehow it broke my own heart.

*

When we undressed for bed Michael was a little less careful about keeping his back turned to me throughout the whole process. There were a couple of moments when, by chance, he half turned towards me as he deposited his shucked garments on the chair beside his bed. On those occasions I saw his cock. It was long, as I'd always imagined it to be, and its foreskin hung like an elegant tassel beyond its tip – like Timmy's did. But the whole thing was nearly twice as big as Timmy's was. Although it was hanging slackly like some exotic flower or fruit, it did flick out towards me slightly as he turned his body, and that had a bit of an impact, I must admit.

In half turning himself in this way, whether by

accident or not, Michael of course had a chance to glimpse my cock. Also slackly hanging, and not as big as his (though with an equally pretty foreskinned tip) it was unlikely to make the same impression on him, my straight best mate, as his had done on me. Naked, we climbed into our separate beds.

After the lights were out and we'd said goodnight I was surprised to hear Michael start up a new conversation in the dark. Perhaps I shouldn't have been. We'd drunk quite a bit out on the pavement by the beach and were both tipsy enough to want to talk late. 'Do you find Tyler beautiful?' he asked.

'I do, of course,' I said. I wanted to add, 'I also find your son beautiful and I find you beautiful,' but fortunately I wasn't quite tipsy enough to do that.

'So do I,' said Michael.

I waited for a second or two, thinking he might add to that, but he did not. So I said, 'Nothing wrong with that. I know beauty is in the eye of the beholder, but sometimes you can see it as a more or less objective fact. Michelangelo's David is a beautiful thing: you don't need to be gay to notice that.'

'What did you think of those two guys wanking each other off in front of us this afternoon?' Michael asked.

'Did I think them beautiful?' I queried. 'I thought they had nice legs and so on. To be honest I didn't notice their faces all that much. I was too busy looking at what they were doing with each other's cocks.'

'Yeah,' said Michael. 'You wouldn't need to be gay to find your attention caught by that.'

'True,' I said.

'Or for it to make you horny.'

'Indeed,' I said. 'It certainly made me horny.'

'Me too,' Michael said.

'I still am,' I said.

Michael gave a sort of dark chuckle. 'Me too, if I'm honest.'

'I haven't done anything about it,' I said mischievously. I was starting to get stiff under the duvet. 'I thought about it when I had a shower earlier...'

'But you didn't go for it...'

'No,' I said. 'What about you?' I was feeling a delicious tingle running down my arms as we carried on this conversation. I was finding it difficult to breathe.

'No,' Michael said. 'Ditto... Except for jumping into the water...'

'I nearly joined you... As for when I was in the shower ... mmm ... well, I was tempted but, well, I couldn't help wondering, like you do, what opportunities might present themselves later.'

'Like you do,' echoed Michael. 'Maybe we'll take up

those boys' offer of a drink tomorrow…' (I'd mentioned their invitation to Michael earlier.)

'That wasn't quite what I was thinking about,' I said.

'Maybe neither was I,' said Michael.

There was a long and very intense silence. I thought hard about taking the biggest gamble of my life. I thought about getting out of bed, walking across to Michael's and feeling for his cock – I knew damn well that it would be stiff by now – through the bedclothes. The last time I'd grabbed his cock that had nearly scuppered our friendship. Did I dare to repeat that near-disaster? Perhaps things were different now, as Tyler had suggested. But he was only a kid still. What did he know about things so difficult and complex?

As I lay thinking, my heart began to pound with anxiety, not just with excitement… Was I about to make a leap in the dark that could result in a tragedy of a landing? … Or was this moment a chance of a lifetime that if not taken might lead to a lifetime of regret on my part if no-one else's? … I heard a movement coming from the direction of Michael's bed. Was he starting to wank beneath the duvet? If so, what should my response be? Walk across and join him, or join him at a distance, jerking off – with just enough noise to make him aware what I was doing – under my own duvet?

I gasped in shock. A hand had alighted on my belly. I felt it through the duvet, and the hand felt my belly. 'Sorry, mate,' said Michael's voice. 'I was on the way to the toilct. Got disoriented in the darkness…' But his hand stayed where he had placed it.

'That's all right,' I said. 'Very nice, actually.' I reached a hand out from under the bedclothes and aimed it roughly towards him. I didn't know what part of him it might make contact with.

It found his hip-bone. Michael still hadn't taken his hand off my belly, though he hadn't allowed it to explore any further. As though my life depended on it I very carefully caressed his warm hip with my middle finger. Like tickling a trout… Either you would catch it or it would disappear like a flash of quicksilver, never to be seen again.

I heard a tiny gasp of breath escape Michael. He didn't move for a moment. Then very slowly his hand glided down my belly till it encountered the ridge of my dick. Very tentatively he clasped what he could of it with his fingers through the blanket.

I slid my own hand across from his hip-bone to his groin area. It was warm and smooth at first, then it began to be furry. He helped me by swinging his hips a little way towards me.

I found the base of his cock with my finger-tips then worked my whole hand up and around it. Up did mean up, quite literally. in this instance. His long silky penis was pointing nearly vertically towards the ceiling.

By now Michael was beginning to squeeze my dick in a series of slow pulses. It felt like it does when a cat starts to knead your belly regularly before settling down on it. I said, 'Get in with me.' The words came out as a whisper.

Adam Wye

NINETEEN

We did hear the boys come back that night. But we took no notice.

In the morning we were awoken by Tyler. He came in without knocking, and without a stitch of clothing covering him. The first thing we knew was his bouncing onto the bed, leaping face down upon the two of us as we lay asleep – and a bit uncomfortably entangled in an embrace that had lasted since we'd both fallen asleep around four o'clock. His tough, modest-sized, pointed erection jabbed at us both alternately as he tousled our two heads and kissed first one and then the other of us like an excited puppy.

'Tyler…' protested Michael groggily as he began to surface from his sleep. 'What the fuck…?'

'Just saying good morning nicely,' Tyler said. 'Welcoming you to the gay world. Welcoming you to your new life…'

'Ty,' I said. 'Do please shut up.'

'For God's sake!' said Michael, unwrapping himself from me and nearly tipping the naked Tyler off the bed by accident in the process.

Trying to piece things together in my befuddled state I said, 'Were you expecting   to   find   us   in   the   same

193

bed?'

'Timmy came in to wake you half an hour ago,' Ty told us. 'Saw you both in bed together and tiptoed away again. A minute ago, with still no sign of life from you, he dared me to come and wake you up myself.'

'What?' I asked 'Naked and with a hard-on?'

'Actually, that bit I dared myself.' Tyler pulled himself up from our two torsos and rearranged himself in a sitting position across our two pairs of legs. 'You two don't half have bony knees,' he said.

'Everybody has,' I said. 'As you'll discover every time you're silly enough to try and sit on them.'

The door opened and Timmy appeared, slightly more decently attired than Ty was, in a pair of very short shorts. 'Dad,' he said, '...and Will. It's nearly twelve o'clock...'

*

While we were sitting outside our pavement café over breakfast – if it wasn't too late to call it breakfast – I received a text. It was from Gary. I knew he'd been due to return to England from America the previous day. He had announced the fact on Facebook. But his news this morning was a dismaying shock. *Leaving the airport terminal yesterday in search of a taxi I looked left instead of right (I'd got used the weird custom they have of driving on the right in New York) and was hit by a car. I'm not on the critical list but all the same I'm in St*

Thomas's with a broken arm and ribs...

'Oh my God,' I said. I showed the others Gary's text. They were all suitably gobsmacked. 'Shit,' I said. 'I may have to go back to England. He doesn't have any family...'

'Will, wait,' said Timmy. 'Don't get into a panic. You've got a friend at St Thomas's. Simon. Your doctor friend...'

'Late-night gay pub pick-up you mean,' said Michael deadpan and with a poker face. But then he went on more animatedly and in a more serious tone of voice, 'Simon's been to Gary's house you told me. Shared his sofa with you...'

'He remarked on the house,' I interrupted. 'Said it was a very nice one.'

'Then let him return Gary's favour,' said Michael. 'You need to phone this Simon character, or text him, and get him to go and find Gary. Get Simon to look after him. There's no need for you to up sticks and go back to England.'

Michael's suggestion came as a huge relief. After last night's unexpected turn of events the last thing I wanted was to leave Michael's side at this moment. Not least because I was worried that he might have regrets about things or change his mind about them in my absence. I texted Simon there and then. He answered at once. He promised to find Gary on the wards during his next break, and to look after him on my behalf. *As a proxy friend,* he said. Only then did I reply to Gary's text. I told him to expect Simon shortly. He was to text me if Simon hadn't materialised within an hour or two. If Simon didn't deliver, I typed, I would be at Gary's side the next day, and that was a promise.

The boys said they wanted to spend the afternoon among the dunes again. I could see from Michael's face that he was torn between two incompatible wishes. By now he very much wanted to go there himself with me, have sex with me there and see for himself what went on there. But equally, he very much *didn't* want to have public sex with me in sight of his own son – and he didn't want to see his son having sex with Tyler. I fully understood his feelings. Much as I for my part found the idea of that particular four-person scenario titillating, I was not Timmy's father. Or even Tyler's…

Michael turned to me. 'What do you suggest we do with the afternoon? Actually – what would you like to do with the afternoon?'

'I'll take you on a bus ride,' I said. 'Show you another bit of the island. If I have to go back to London tomorrow … at least you'll know your way around a bit.'

The suggestion might have surprised him. It was a bit counter-intuitive perhaps, given that it didn't seem to involve opportunities for sex, and that Michael and I had only just discovered the pleasures of sex between us. I watched Michael's face as he considered my idea. I think that what came into his mind was what had just swum into mine: the thought or feeling than had made me suggest what I did. That it wasn't only the sexual attraction between us that we were just beginning to acknowledge. That it was also something else. Something that ran deeper than the joys of sex.

I saw Michael's head nod slowly. 'Yes,' he said then. 'I'd like that.' He turned to the others. 'You two OK for cash?' And he sorted things out with his son and Tyler, and we arranged where and when we'd meet up when we were back from our trip.

*

Sitting next to Michael on the plane two days before I had wanted to stroke his thigh alongside mine but hadn't dared to. Now, on a bouncing Canary Island bus I did just that. He returned the compliment and neither of us cared if other passengers saw us or if they didn't, or what they thought about it if they did.

Our destination was Puerto de Mogan, a little way around the southern tip of the island's coast-line. The road led up and down through hills that had been carved into terraces by hungrier, more desperate generations of islanders over the centuries. Now that tourism provided a slightly easier source of income than growing vegetables on rocky slopes the terraces were mostly abandoned. But even in their overgrown state they remained beautiful and inspiring. The sea rose and fell on the other side of us as the bus ground its way up the hills and rattled down the valleys.

Puerto de Mogan was a charming mixture of fishing port and holiday resort. There was an area of intersecting canals, bordered with newly painted houses. Bright bougainvillea and trumpet vine climbed and dangled everywhere, their fallen petals flecking the water's surface with colour. We stopped for a glass of wine and an omelette where tables were set out in a garden. A pair of hoopoes, bright pink and zebra-striped, had a nest in a tree above us and flew to and fro charmingly, as if their prettiness was part of the service.

'You're not going to interrogate me, are you?' said Michael as we eyeballed each other fondly across the garden dining-table. 'About how gay I am, or how bisexual, or when I knew...? Or why I didn't do anything about it?'

'No,' I said. 'None of that matters. You'll tell me at some point in the future if you find you want to. And if you don't...' I shrugged. 'No problem.'

The smile that Michael gave me was worth a thousand confessions and explanations.

An email came through on my phone. It was from Simon. *Writing on behalf of Gary. He's doing fine. I'm going to his place this evening to bring back some of his things. He'll be out of hosp in two days. I'll be staying at his for a week or two to help him do cooking and washing while he's still one-handed. He says, no need for you to come over. Love, Simon xx*

I'd no sooner relayed this good news to Michael (he

was as relieved as I was that I wouldn't have to depart for London the next morning) than I got a one-handed text from Gary. *Tks f yr concern & f sending me Simon. Love, Gary.* I showed this to Michael. 'Hmm,' he said approvingly. 'You seem to have got a lot of things sorted.' I didn't ask him to list them.

We took a walk around one arm of the fishing harbour. On one side of us the open Atlantic was tough and grainy, on the other side the sheltered water of the harbour was clear and sparkling with fish waving their tails at us from just below the surface. But the highlight of the walk was the sight of a young and muscular fisherman – perhaps about eighteen years old – who was wearing nothing but skin-tight shorts through which the contours of his cock and balls were clearly discernible. He was unloading fish from the deck of a boat and packing it into polystyrene boxes. On the pretext of admiring the catch Michael and I stopped to watch him.

'That knocks most of the naked hunks around Maspalomas into a cocked hat,' said Michael appreciatively. I agreed with him. I also realised that his comment revealed the solidity of his gayness. He not only fancied me, he also fancied other men and boys... I remembered how he'd hinted that he fancied Tyler. Oddly enough I found all this reassuring.

We walked to the very end of the harbour arm. There was nobody near us. Just seagulls and the salty breeze. Abruptly Michael turned to face me He took my head in his hands and pulled my lips towards his. A second later I found myself welcoming his tongue into my mouth.

With a sense of wonder – for was this not the man who'd said he wouldn't kiss me till I was on my death bed? – I slid my tongue into his.

*

'You're not going to interrogate me, are you?' I asked.

'About what?' Michael's beautiful face softened into a smile.

'About when I began to fall in love with you, and how and why?'

'No,' he said. 'People who live in glass houses…' He smiled, then chuckled. 'It'll come out in its own time, no doubt. Though only if or when you want it to. But we've got time. We've got the rest of our lives.'

I could read a lot into that. And I did. Michael saw us as having a future together. Some sort of future. What kind of future, though… It was a bit soon to speculate. We were next-door neighbours. Would we continue as neighbours, but neighbours who added a few moments of sex to our weekly evening drink, keeping the rest of our lives separate and hiding the truth about our relationship from our other neighbours, our families, and the people in the pub? Or would we move in together, pooling our lives and reputations, sharing one of our houses and selling the other one or renting it out? My thoughts were running much too far ahead. It was way too soon to speculate. I looked at Michael and gave him an answering smile. 'The rest of our lives,' I said. 'I like that.' I felt a sting in my eyes and a tightening of the throat.

We were spending our third evening as we had spent the first two. Following dinner and the disappearance of Timmy and Ty to the fleshpots of the Yumbo Centre, we were sitting outside our regular bar by the beach. From the darkness beyond the promenade lights the faint white lines of surf rolled in and disappeared with a sigh that sounded all too human. Above us the palm fronds interlaced and the night's stars appeared to dangle between them like pendant jewels and necklaces. Two nights ago we'd been a pair of friends. Last night the friendly staff had taken us, misguidedly, for a pair of lovers. Tonight the staff were wonderfully, gloriously, right.

Last night we had fallen upon each other's bodies as soon as Michael had climbed into my bed. We'd sucked each other's nipples, dug fingers into each other's buttocks and thighs. We'd explored each other's arseholes with our fingers. We'd twisted round each other till we were nose to tail and swallowed each other's dicks. I have to admit that Michael's was one of the more difficult, on account of its length, that I'd ever tried to accommodate in my mouth. In the end we'd come, lying tummy against tummy, hands working at each other's cocks, Michael lying on top. An hour and a half later we repeated the whole performance almost exactly, climaxing in the same way, though this time with me lying on top.

I wasn't sure when the time would come when Michael decided he wanted to try fucking me – or to let me do him. I didn't intend to hurry things. Perhaps that time would never come (especially for the second of those two pleasures!) It wouldn't matter. When two people love each other the details of what they do together in the way of sex are exactly that – mere details. Even if those details are very nice…

This night we didn't walk straight back from the beachside bar to our bungalow. We walked down the beach towards the infinite darkness of the Atlantic instead, towards the pungent, exciting smells of iodine and salt and the sound of the sighing surf.

We took our shorts and T-shirts off and walked into the water naked except for our flip-flops. We stood knee-deep among the wavelets and held each other tightly as we kissed, rubbing our still flat tummies warmly against each other's. After a moment Michael made a move to break away. 'I need to piss,' he explained.

'Just do it,' I said.

'What? Like this? It'll go all down your leg.'

'That's fine,' I said. 'We're in the sea. We can wash.'

So Michael did, and after a second I joined in, unable not to. But we didn't do it down each other's legs; we pissed up against each other's tummies and chests, for the simple and rather obvious reason that both our cocks had become erect. Though then of course, it did run down our legs. It was a rather wonderful and surprising moment. A bonding experience that was deeply intimate. Our exchanged waterfalls felt pleasantly hot. We continued to grind our bellies and cocks together until we'd run out of juice. Then we crouched down, scooping up surf by the handful and splashing each other fresh and clean with it.

'I haven't done that since I was a small kid,' said Michael as we waded back out of the sea towards our shorts and T-shirts, dimly visible on the sand ahead.

'Neither have I, I think,' I said. Although actually I had. Just once or twice…

TWENTY

Over the next days we relaxed into our new relationship. Our holiday spot was an ideal place to do it. We were just one more gay couple in a whole resort full of gay couples. We had sex in bed every night, of course, and also down on the beach one afternoon when the two boys had gone off somewhere else. Once we masturbated each other on the loungers by the pool in broad daylight, which we thought very brave of us. Needless to say we picked a moment when Timmy and Ty weren't around. We didn't repeat our experiment with watersports, or go any further down that route. Neither did we even attempt to fuck each other yet.

We did have that beer with the other couple we'd seen wanking naked by the poolside. They were a very nice pair. We sat naked alongside them at the poolside bar, getting to know each other a little as we drank. We didn't have sex with them, though, or even touch their cocks, and they didn't touch ours. They too were a new couple. Neither they nor we were prepared to take risks with something so vulnerable and precious as a new relationship.

But then, one day, calamity struck. I knew that the sword of Damocles hung perilously over my head. Gary had warned me of what could happen, what was almost certain to happen, months before – though I knew it anyway, even before that.

For once the four of us – Timmy and Ty, Michael and I – were in a late-night club in the Yumbo Centre: two gay couples out on the razz together. An email came through on Ty's phone. It was from Danny. Ty would have done better to leave reading it till the morning. But he was a little drunk – we all were – and he read it there and then. He read it aloud to us.

'Hi Ty. Late night slightly drunk email. Alone tonight. Hope things going well in Gran Canaria for you and Tim. Me playing with me dick now and remembering the good times we three used to have.' So far, just about OK, though it was already getting close to dangerous ground as far as Michael's listening ears were concerned. At least the nature of those good times had not been exactly spelled out. Had Ty been sober he would have seen the next sentence coming and stopped himself before reading it out. But he wasn't sober; he didn't see it coming; he read it out.

'Remember the time we caught Tim fucking his dad's friend on the beach?' At that point he did stop, horribly aware suddenly of the havoc his carelessness had unleashed. The silence was awful. Timmy's eyes and mine met first. We each saw fear and horror in each other's faces, and for the moment neither of us could speak.

Michael spoke. Before I had time to glance at his face. 'I'm going back to the bungalow,' he said.

'I'm coming with you,' I said. We both sounded distraught.

'Don't,' he said. 'Don't follow me. None of you.' He shouldered his way through the press of bodies and disappeared from sight. Had he finished with something like *Enjoy the rest of your evening* it might, I suppose have been even worse. But not much.

'I'll go after him,' I said. 'Follow at a distance. Make sure he doesn't do anything stupid.'

'Are you sure…?' began Ty.

'Don't worry. I won't try to catch him up. He needs a few minutes to think. I'll let him get to the bungalow first.'

'Do you want us to come with you?' Timmy asked.

'No,' I said. 'Not yet. Play it by ear when you do get back.'

Tyler put one arm round Timmy's shoulder and the other one round my waist. I could feel him shaking. 'I'm so fucking sorry. And so stupid… I've fucked everything up for both of you. And Michael…' His voice began to choke, and tears started to roll down his cheeks.

'It wasn't your fault, Ty,' I said gently. 'None of it was remotely your fault. Now you look after Timmy. He needs you most. See you later … maybe.' I turned and barged my way through the crowd towards the door as Michael had done just a minute earlier.

I didn't see Michael in the streets between the Yumbo

Centre and the bungalow complex. I walked faster in the hope of catching sight of him and had to fight down the beginnings of panic when I did not. But when I got back to our place I saw lights on and my fears for Michael's immediate state of mind and for his safety abated somewhat.

I opened the door. At least he hadn't locked me out. I saw his back view, standing near the sink. Having a drink of water, maybe, making a cup of coffee... At least he hadn't gone into the bedroom and locked the door.

He didn't turn round as I approached him. I came up behind him and put my hands on his waist. I felt his body go rigid. 'Don't touch me,' he said. I took my hands away, though without rushing it. Still with his back to me he said, 'You had sex with Timmy.'

'Yes,' I said.

'You had an affair with him.'

'Yes.' My voice was barely a whisper by this point.

He spun round and faced me. Even now I can't bear to remember the look he had on his face. 'I don't know you,' he said. 'You're not the person I thought you were. You're not the William I thought I knew. You're someone else.'

I felt myself shake all over: the profound hammering shake of a ship that has struck a rock. It was difficult to speak. 'I am the William you've always known,' I said. 'I love you,' I said.

He said nothing in reply to that. There was no change to the expression on his face. He went on slowly, in a low voice, 'You seduced my son behind my back. You had your way with him and deceived me about it.'

'He was eighteen when it started,' I said. 'He wasn't a child. He wasn't under your protection. He was an adult. In legal terms, and in all other respects. I didn't seduce him...' I had to weigh my words carefully. I wasn't going to excuse myself like a coward and say that Timmy started it. 'It just happened. For both of us.'

'He's eighteen,' Michael said. 'Barely that. You're thirty-eight. Think about it. And all the time it was going on ... maybe it's still going on...'

'It isn't. Of course it isn't. We broke up when Tyler and he fell in love...'

'...And all the time it was going on you came into my house, drank my wine and ate my food, I came to yours... And you said nothing about it. Pretended it wasn't going on. Acted with me as if butter wouldn't melt in your mouth. How's Tim? you'd ask. And Timmy this, and Timmy that... And all the time I never guessed. Because you were lying to me with every fibre of your heart.'

I broke apart. Tears fell down my face and I started to sob. I wanted Michael to take me in his arms at that point and make everything all right. But he did not. He could not. I had to recover for myself, without his help, before I could speak. 'I'm sorry,' I said. 'I'm sorry I've hurt you. I'm sorry you're upset and hurt. But I can't be sorry for falling in love with Timmy. Because that's what happened. We both fell in love. Then he fell out of love because he fell in love with someone more suitable. Tyler. Then I fell out of love with him – a bit more slowly – because… Because… Because I was already in love with someone else. Someone who I thought was unattainable. But then, for a brief few days he didn't seem so unattainable. For a few days…' I had to stop for a second. Even after that I could barely mumble. 'These last few days have been the happiest of my life.'

The silence that followed that was agony. I looked at Michael. I could see from his eyes that it was an agony for both of us.

'I'm sorry I deceived you,' I said. 'But I deceived you only in what I didn't say, not in what I did. I still felt terrible about it, even so. But what could I say? What does anyone ever say in that situation? Blurt out that I was having an affair with Timmy? It was a private matter between us. And like I said, he's an adult.'

'He's still my son,' Michael said with vehemence. 'He still needs my protection and my love. He's not like other sons. Not like other people…'

'I know,' I said. 'Because he's yours. He always will be. And he'll always love you – as much as any son ever loved his father – with all his heart – for as long as he lives.'

Michael still stood facing me, in shorts and T-shirt,

rock-like, granite-faced.

'Deceiving people,' I said. 'Who in the world is entirely blameless when it comes to that? You've been knocking off another man's wife.' Michael started. I wondered if he was close to hitting me. At any rate he did not. 'I'm not saying that in a blaming sort of way. These things happen. I'm just stating a fact.'

Before I could state any more facts the door opened and Tyler walked in.

Michael turned abruptly towards Tyler. 'Where's Timmy?' he asked, with something like panic in his voice.

'I made him stay outside,' said Tyler. 'He's fine. He's sitting by the poolside under the lights. He won't come to any harm for five minutes. But I needed to face the music. I needed to face up to you first.' This was directed at Michael. I wasn't included in it.

'What do you mean?' Michael asked.

'I need to apologise for reading out that stupid email. I wasn't thinking straight. I should have kept it to myself. But there's more than that…'

'Let's all sit down,' Michael said. He spread his arms like someone shepherding geese and shooed us towards the living-room space.

We arranged ourselves among the chairs there. Then Ty went on. 'I've been having sex with Timmy for years. Sex of a sort. It was a kids' thing at first. And private. Later I knew about Timmy and Will…' He turned to me. 'Are you OK if I go on with this?'

'Yes,' I said in a husk of a voice.

'Timmy moved away from me – emotionally, I mean, nearly a year ago. It was getting difficult for him. For both of us. The gay thing, I mean. Then he fell in love with Will. He's told me all this. In part because he – Will, I mean – was an older man and it seemed safe… Sorry, Will…'

'It's OK,' I said.

'Will didn't seduce Timmy, if that's what you're thinking, Michael. Timmy wanted it too. And he's told me – just now – that he's OK with me telling you this. The thing is that now … well, the two of you seem to have found each other … and it all seemed perfect … Timmy and I had found each other again … and you two are just so right for each other…' At that point Ty's adult poise, his amazing cool and calm, deserted him and the tears sprang.

I stood up. 'I think I'd better go out and see to Timmy,' I said. 'If that's OK with both of you?' Michael and Ty both nodded their heads. 'I'll let the two of you talk a bit longer.' I gave Ty's shoulder a supportive tweak on my way out.

Timmy was sitting on the edge of one of the sun-loungers. There was enough lighting from the subdued floodlights to see his silhouette. I sat down next to him.

'It's OK, Timmy, I said.

For a moment he sat there motionless, not acknowledging my arrival. Then he said, 'Can you put your arm around me?' Of course I did.

'I was about to ask you if I could do that,' I said. 'You beat me to it.'

'You must think I'm a total shit,' Timmy said.

I was taken aback. 'Why would I think that?'

'The way I treated you. One minute I was in love with you, the next...'

'Don't think about it,' I said. 'There was no way it could have worked out for us. You were young ... you still are ...and I was deluding myself.'

'You weren't,' said Timmy. He put his hand on my thigh and clamped it tight. 'It was real for both of us.'

'OK,' I said. 'Yes, it was.'

'I'm sorry,' Timmy said.

I said, 'There's nothing to be sorry about.'

'I don't know what I'm going to say to dad,' said Timmy. 'I'm scared.'

'You know what, Timmy?' I said. 'All of us go on through life being scared of pretty well everything. That's something that adults hardly ever tell the kids.

We pretend we're not scared. We get on with life. Do you know something?'

'What?' Timmy asked.

'You told me about what you felt for me – I mean that I might be hurt – before you talked about being scared to talk to Michael. That was a big thing. Do you realise that? I'll tell your dad – if we're still having conversations – that he's got a big brave son with a big heart. That his son is someone who doesn't put himself first but thinks of others' pain before his own.'

'That's a bit… I mean, it's difficult to take that last bit in… I guess it was a compliment. I'll have to unravel it later. But…' He put his own arm around me at this point and nuzzled his head against mine, and his shoulder, his thigh, his knee… 'I mean, I've been lucky to find Tyler. Really find him, I mean. But you've got dad, haven't you? I mean, you really have. Despite tonight's spat…'

'Oh God, Timmy,' I said. I clasped him tight. 'I don't know. I wanted that. I hoped I had… It's up to him, though. I'm not sure, after what's been said tonight, that he wants me.'

'Of course he does,' Timmy said sturdily. 'He wouldn't have made the fuss he did tonight if he wasn't head-over-heels in love with you…'

'Whoa, whoa…' I said.

'Just as you are with him,' Timmy went on, ignoring my doubt. 'You have been for years. Even while Aidan was still alive you were a little bit in love with dad. I could see that. It's very unlikely that dad couldn't…'

'I don't know…' I began. But at that moment Michael and Ty walked out from the bungalow together and came towards us. They were not arm in arm, they were not holding hands. They just walked side by side like friends do.

Michael made a beeline for me. At first I couldn't see his face. He was silhouetted for a moment by a light behind him which shone through his ears and made them glow red like a car's tail lights. When his face was illuminated more normally again I could see that he wasn't smiling. He took hold of my two hands and gently pulled me to my feet. Then he put his arms around me and held me tight. I nuzzled my head against his neck. From just behind my ear and just above it I heard the whisper of his voice. 'I'm sorry,' it said.

'I'm sorry,' I said.

*

We didn't do anything in the way of sex when we got to bed. We didn't even talk very much. Though Michael did say at one point, 'I think I just had a lecture on the meaning of love from an eighteen-year-old kid.'

'I think perhaps I did too,' I said.

We both cried a bit as we lay in each others arms, consoling each other; sharing the knowledge that there is no love without pain; that there is no belonging to another human being without moments of jealousy; that a life in which we don't get hurt sometimes by those who love us most and whom we love most is no life at all but just a faint copy of what life is. Holding each other, knowing that we needed each other, knowing that we loved each other, we rocked each other gently to sleep.

TWENTY-ONE

I wasn't going to suggest it. The idea would have to come from Michael or it wouldn't happen at all. But it did come from Michael. One day when the two youngsters had taken the bus up the coast to see the island's capital, Las Palmas, Michael and I traipsed along the beach towards the dunes – wearing shorts, T-shirts and flip-flops and carrying the trusty spare blanket from the cupboard. It had done sterling service for the younger couple in protecting them against sand in the works, and we trusted it would do the same for us.

Getting to the dunes involved quite a trek. At first sight the area appeared devoid of life but soon we found every sheltered hollow in the square mile of undulating sand contained at least one male figure, if not two or sometimes three, and every one of them either fully naked or else clad in only a T-shirt and so still displaying their wares in terms of cocks and balls and thighs.

'I've never seen so many cocks in one place,' said Michael as we walked along. 'Actually I don't think I've ever seen this many cocks in my entire life.'

'Welcome to the dunes of Maspalomas,' I said. 'And have you noticed that no two pricks are quite the same? Like snowflakes, each one is slightly different.'

'I must remember that,' Michael said. We came at last to an unoccupied dip in the dunes and spread our blanket in it.

'I've never fucked a man before,' Michael said when we'd taken our scant clothing off.

'And I've never fucked a woman,' I said. 'But the mechanics are much the same, even if the plumbing's a bit different.'

'I've never... How to put this daintily...' Michael hesitated, then decided to abandon the attempt. 'I've never fucked a woman in the arse.'

'It's a tighter fit than round at the front, I'm told,' I said. 'Best use a finger first. Help me to relax...' I could see from the thoughtful expression on his face that Michael was realising I must have taught his son this.

He wanted to do it with me on my back, looking into my brown eyes – eyes his son had surprisingly described as resembling dark cherries – while I looked into his blue-as-the-sky eyes and the blue-as-his-eyes sky behind his head.

I felt an unanticipated moment of fright just before he entered me with his long penis. It was probably the longest one I'd ever been fucked with, even if it wasn't exceptionally thick. 'I know it's not my first time,' I said. 'But be gentle with me.'

'I'll try my best,' he said. Then, his finger exercise over and done with, he entered me slowly and surely, pushing himself smoothly all the way in, up to the hilt, as if he'd been born for   this moment.

I'd managed to relax completely, I discovered. My moment of anxiety had been unwarranted. I felt him, watched him, surge into me, pull back, surge in again, like the waves that rolled sighing, smooth and regular, along the beach.

He didn't touch my cock as he rode me, though he looked at it often as well as at my face. 'Are you OK?' he asked me twice, and I said yes both times.

'Yes,' he said. 'You look it. There's a smile on your face.'

'And on yours,' I said.

'I think I'm coming,' he said suddenly. There was a bit of surprise in his voice. Then I felt his prick thicken and pulse inside me and his whole body tensed and bucked. His face contorted for a second or two and then relaxed. He crumpled on top of me. 'I've come,' he said.

I said, 'I know you have.' And then the most amazing thing happened to me. 'Hey, I'm coming too,' I said.

Michael raised himself from my chest just enough so that he could peer down at my orgasming penis. We both saw my ejaculate trickling slowly out. 'I'll help it along a bit,' Michael said. He took my slowly streaming dick into his hand and wanked the remainder of my spunk out. Then, when he was quite sure I'd finished he lay back down on my chest again, bathing his tummy against my warm sticky mess.

'I've never done that before,' I said. 'Come without

being touched while being fucked.' I didn't tell him that Timmy had. There are some things you just don't tell people's parents.

'First time for everything,' said Michael. His long rod was still inside me. He showed no sign of wanting to take it out. He rubbed at the side of my head with his hands so that I heard my hair crackle. Then he kissed me on the lips. 'I love you,' he said softly.

'I love you too,' I said.

*

There was a first time for something else too. I didn't know for certain if there would be, but there was. It happened a couple of weeks after we returned to England. We both had an afternoon off work on the same day. We were sunbathing in the garden naked, while Timmy and Ty had gone off together into town. Michael said it. Quite suddenly. Quite simply. 'I'd like you to fuck me. If you'd like that.'

'I would,' I said. We both had hard-ons, as we usually did when we were lying around naked together, or playing with each other. I've written *the garden* but we now actually owned two gardens between us. That day we were in the one that was officially Michael's. So I fucked Michael for the first time ever beneath the tree, in approximately the same spot, where Timmy had had his first miniature ejaculation about five years before. Though I decided not to tell Michael that.

I made sure to take my time about getting him

relaxed. Plenty of licking, plenty of lube and plenty of finger work. Michael went face-down on the grass. He said he wanted it that way, first time round anyway. And my patience paid off. He was wonderfully, surprisingly, easy to get into. Surprisingly, because although my prick wasn't as big as his was it wasn't a small one by most people's standards. I had the dream of a fuck with him, and came ecstatically while he rubbed his own cock beneath his belly on the grass. He didn't come while he was being fucked. (I hadn't spontaneously done so either since that first time being fucked by him: that extraordinary event had proved to be a one-off.) But after I'd pulled out of him he rolled onto his back and I brought him off in a leisurely way with my fist, while tickling his small tight balls and the area just behind them with my free hand. The tickling made him giggle at first, and then it made him squirt – which he did in great abundance, all up over his chest. After which I lay on top of him and we cuddled each other in it. Till it dried, and then we went in and showered together, enjoying the pleasure of cleaning each other off…

*

A year has passed since then. Timmy and Ty are still together. At university. They were lucky enough to be accepted by the same one, Brighton, which was exactly what they'd both wanted but hardly dared to hope. During their vacation time they live mostly with us.

And where do we live? Well, that depends. We've kept both houses, and live for a few months at a time together in one or other of them while renting the other one out. It's quite fun alternating in this way every six months or so: the change of scene is good for us.

Going to sleep together every night, whichever master bedroom we happen to be occupying at the time, is one of the highlights of our day. The other one is waking up together every morning: seeing the other's face and smiling at each other if we wake simultaneously – or else waking Michael with a kiss, or being woken by his kiss and his chuckling murmur of, 'I love you,' if one of us wakes up first.

Michael has had the difficult task of explaining to his various girlfriends that he is no longer in the market for heterosexual intercourse. That he's found that he is closer to the gay end of the spectrum than he'd realised, is in a relationship with a man they have been on nodding terms with for a year or two – his next-door neighbour – and that he and I are now sexually exclusive. For me the task has been easier. There was only Simon who required any kind of explanation. And he took it on board very easily – and probably with a feeling of relief. After all, he is himself now part of an exclusive double act with Gary. Having moved in to his mews house with him when Gary was convalescing a year ago from his rib-breaking, arm-wrenching accident, Simon has never moved out. The two of them seem set for the long haul, just as Michael and I are – and as Timmy and Ty seem to be.

Timmy and his father are still very close. I've seldom seen a father and son relationship quite like it, seldom seen one that is quite so lovely and so loving. And I'm very close to Tyler. But there's no question of sex between us. We all hug a lot, and kiss, and talk quite intimately about some things. But I don't have sex with Tyler or – these days – with Timmy. Nor does Michael. I mean by that that he doesn't have sex with Ty. That he doesn't have sex with Timmy … well I hardly need to say that he doesn't do that.

The Green Dragon, our local pub, turned out to be a pushover. When Michael and I started going in there as a couple – and sometimes with Timmy and Tyler, which made two new gay couples in the village at a stroke… Well, nobody turned a hair, which surprised us almost more than anything else that has happened. Even the toughest old farming types said things like, 'High time you two got it together,' and, 'Good on yer, guys.'

I've written that that surprised us almost more than anything else. The biggest surprise by far, though, is that I've ended up with Michael – a dream I'd thought impossible, and for years had never dared to hope might come true. And that Michael, having ended up with me, likes it that way and says he can now no longer imagine wanting anything else. That's the biggest surprise of all. And by far the best and loveliest.

THE END

****

Adam Wye

Other novels by Adam Wye.

Love in Venice

Gay in Moscow

Adam Wye is a pen name of the British author
Anthony McDonald

All Adam Wye and Anthony McDonald titles are
available as Kindle ebooks and as paperbacks from
Amazon.

www.anthonymcdonald.co.uk

Manufactured by Amazon.ca
Bolton, ON